INTO THE PAST

WRITTEN BY:

SHAMIKA HILL

DEDICATION

I dedicate this book to my grandparents whom I lost just before and during the creation of this book. Inez and Wilbur Hill, and Papa Bob, aka Robert Turner. Thank you for all the conversations we had, the laughs we shared, the stories you've told, and the teachings you taught. I will always cherish the wonderful memories we shared. There is not a day that goes by that I don't think about you. I didn't know what a heartbreak felt like until the day you went home to be with the Lord, yet I still thank God for all the wonderful years he allowed us to have. I know we will be together again one day but until then rest in heavenly piece. I love you always

ACKNOWLEDGMENTS

First, I would like to give glory and thanks to God because without him and his strength, none of this would be possible.

To my grandparents Erma Turner and Oscar Long, thank you for the encouragement and support. Our family has been through a lot during the writing of this book, and that didn't stop you from calling me every night to check on me and tell me how proud you are of me.

To my parents Kathy and Carl Hill, thank you so much for pushing me to get this story out. I doubted myself so many times, I complained to you how both of you were blessed with many gifts and talents, and that you didn't pass any of it down to me. Thank you both for helping me to realize that I came from a family of writers. Thank you both for pushing me to finish this book through all the hurt, pain and happiness that we have experienced this year.

Daddy, you kept telling me to make it explode. I hope you can feel the heat. Thanks so much for your love, encouragement and support. I love you both with all my heart

To my wonderful husband Brian Epps, you are my rock. You carry me at times I can't carry myself. Thank you so much for all your prayers, your encouragement, and your support. I thank God for you every day. You're a wonderful husband and father. Love you bae!

To my mother-in-law Rene Fields, I know you live on the east coast, but you certainly didn't let that stop you from calling every Saturday, to check on us and find out my progress on my book. You let me know how proud you are of me, and how you couldn't wait to read my first book. Thank you for standing by me and giving me the push, I needed as well. Love you

To my beautiful children, Kyla, Ayden, Zaynen,

and little Karli Epps. You four are my world. You little blessings kept me going. I love you more than life itself. Thank you for always asking me to read chapters to you, thank you for the excitement you showed when it came to the characters of my book. Kyla thank you for giving my book a title. Kids get bored fast, and the fact that you guys showed so much interest in my book at a young age gave me the fire I needed to keep going. All ways remember to reach for the stars. Keep God in your life because through him, all things are possible.

To my sisters, La Shondra Crittenden, Nicole Stephens, and Jada Hill, you ladies rock! Thank you for all the feedback, and your support and encouragement. Nicole the way I hear you talking about my book puts a smile on my face, it gave me the drive I needed to keep going when I was starting to doubt myself. I love you guys to the moon and back.

To my brothers in law Demetri Stephens and

Jimmie Crittenden. You keep the encouragement going. Your support through this journey was strong. Thank you for all the advice you gave.

Sherene-Holly Cain and I'munique Stephens, you are certainly a blessing. Thank you for taking me under your wing and sculpting me to be a better writer. Thanks for all the advice, and education that you are still providing me. I'm grateful for you pushing me and making sure I reached my deadline. Because of you I get to turn my dream to life.

To all the Dream2Life team. Thank you all for all the encouragement, prayers, and support.

I am truly blessed to have so many people in my corner. If I forgot to mention anyone, please forgive me. Charge it to my brain, not my heart.

1

My name is Brielle Taylor and I always make dumb decisions. Take today, for instance. It's not enough that I came all the way to Mississippi one week early to help prepare for our annual Taylor family reunion, I just had to offer to take my cousin shopping for a last-minute supply run. To make matters worse, it's raining, and the sun went down an hour ago.

"OMG! CeCe, did you really use all the battery in my phone?" I yelled at my cousin after tossing my cell phone in the cup holder. "You left me with two percent on my battery! I can't use the GPS on a two percent charge," I said, frustrated.

CeCe smacked her lips and rolled her eyes, looking out the passenger side window. "Sorry," she said with an attitude.

"I'm addicted to TikTok… and Instagram…

Snapchat, oh and Facebook. Well, not so much Facebook."

"Omg, really! I didn't even have those apps on my phone. I can't believe you not only used my phone without my permission, but you also downloaded apps!" I stated, still frustrated.

"Oh, and this game, have you ever played—"

"Did you not just hear what I said? You downloaded a game on my phone too," I cut her off, even more annoyed. "How were you doing all that while we were talking, shopping, and tugging bags around all day? I didn't even know you had my phone."

I had bought a new phone just before making the journey to Mississippi. I hadn't had a chance to set up a pin just yet. I planned on doing that as soon as I was able to charge it.

"What can I say? I'm awesome at multitasking,"

2

she stated.

"Well, obviously, not that good. Had you been watching where you were going, you wouldn't have tripped over the curb, dropped your phone, and broke it," I gloated.

"It's ok." She shrugged her shoulders. "I'll just take donations at the family reunion tomorrow," she said with a smirk on her face. "It was time for an upgrade anyway."

I sighed and shook my head. "Well. Don't come to me with a collection cup."

She just gave me a slight laugh and shrugged her shoulders. Typical CeCe. Nothing ever really worried her. Both CeCe and I were twenty-one years old. I loved my cousin but, lately, she'd been getting on my nerves. I felt like she didn't take things seriously. I worked and went to school fulltime. CeCe went to school, but she refused to get a job. She expected everyone to pay her way. It seemed like I was growing up, and she was still sixteen.

I always thought CeCe was pretty. She worked out regularly, so she was very toned. She's 5'3 and had the pretty green eyes that ran in the Taylor family. Her eyes complemented her cinnamon-colored skin tone. She would make the perfect model. Surprisingly, that's not what she wanted to do.

CeCe made it a point to always be picture ready. She wore a red crop top sweater with black, high-waisted cut-up skinny jeans, and black slouch boots that hugged her calves. Her long wavy hair was in a tight ponytail. You would never catch her without her edges laid. She only went by the name CeCe. I didn't think anyone knew her name was Ciera except for her family.

I, on the other hand, was the complete opposite. I was taller than CeCe. I was 5'5. I hated social media. I dressed more for comfort and not for the camera, however, I did like an occasional game. My go-to game right now was Homescapes. I had on a black, cotton long-sleeve shirt,

INTO THE PAST

black and white tie-dye sweatpants, and my black high-top Nike sneakers. I wore my braided hair in a high bun. Unlike CeCe, I wasn't gifted with the family trademark. Instead of the beautiful green eyes that ran in the family, I was given beautiful hazel eyes that paired well with my milk chocolate skin color. Hazel eyes were common in my family as well, but the green eyes were more dominant.

"Do you remember how to get to Aunt Gracie's house from here?" I asked CeCe, hoping that something looked familiar to her. Honestly, I didn't even know why I asked her. Obviously, her eyes were glued to my phone the whole time I was driving.

"No, it's so dark, I can barely make anything out and this rain isn't helping."

"I know, it's really coming down. I had to have made a wrong turn somewhere. I don't see not one person that I could ask for directions," I said, starting to feel worried. We were on a two-lane road with nothing but forest around us. There were no streetlights around us. The only lights we had was from our headlights.

"I'm going to have to pull over. We'll have to either wait this storm out or wait for daylight. If we keep going, we could end up in trouble."

"The way I see it, we're in trouble either way. I'm sure Aunt Gracie has tried to call us by now. We told her we'll be back by six o'clock, and it's almost nine-thirty. I'm sure the whole family knows we are missing right now," CeCe said worriedly.

"Yeah, I can't imagine how worried they are. I guess you can say we have officially ruined this year's Taylor family reunion. Look! I think that's a dirt road up ahead to the right. We can pull over and wait there for the rain to pass or wait till morning."

CeCe turned around to look at the road behind us.

"Well, nobody is following us… yeah, go ahead and turn down the dirt road; it's better than sitting on the side of the road where we can easily be spotted."

I pull onto the dirt road; it went nowhere. It's a dead end. There was an old split rail fence that wrapped around the back end of the road. I parked on the side of the rail and turn the car off. CeCe and I both look around. We were surrounded by forest and complete darkness once the head lights were off.

"This is crazy; I really feel like we are in the middle of a scary movie! You can't tell me you don't feel just a little scared," CeCe said.

"Yea, but we're ok. There are no cars, no houses, absolutely nobody around us. We're safe," I assured her. In a way, I think I was trying to make myself feel better.

CeCe leaned her seat back, as I stared out the driver's side window. "Well, I'm about to try to get some sleep. Good thing we brought our jackets! Make sure the doors are locked," CeCe said.

With that, I locked the door and leaned my seat back as well. Sleep came quick with the sound of the rain. I woke up to the sunlight blinding me. The rain had stopped. I picked up my phone to glance at the time, then remembered my phone was dead. I turned the car on to look at the time. It was 7:05 a.m. I leaned my seat up and tried to shake CeCe awake. She was the hardest sleeper I'd ever met. I shook her once more.

CeCe! I'm going to the bathroom. I'll be back."

"Uh huh," she replied and turned her back to me.

As soon as I opened the door, the cold morning air hit me. I shivered as I zipped up my jacket. Even though it was wet and muddy outside, it was beautiful. There were tall tress all around. I loved the smell of rain, wet tree trunk and flowers. The smell of the forest relaxed me. The ground was covered in branches and fallen leaves of different colors. I could hear the leaves blowing in the wind. I heard the birds chirping and some frogs croaking.

I walked a few feet in the direction of the frogs. It was not that I wanted to see one; it was just the sound of their croaking was so mesmerizing. I noticed a small dirt trail off to the side. Forgetting that I had to relieve myself, I turned to walk down the dirt trail, taking in all the beauty that surrounded me. As I was walking, I felt this sharp burst of energy that knocked the breath out of my body. My whole body was tingling, and I felt lightheaded. I kneeled to balance myself. The sensation I was feeling only seemed to last a few seconds.

"What in the world was that?" I asked out loud.

Startled, I stood up straight and looked around. Shaking my head, I decided I must be hungry. The last time I ate was breakfast yesterday morning. I kept walking down the trail. After passing a bunch of tall trees, the land turned

flat. There was an open field with an old wooden house

sitting in the middle. It was a square house, with one

window in the front next to a door. There were a few steps

that led from the door to the ground. The house sat on a

platform. I could tell the house was abandoned. I felt like

my body was moving on its own.

I walked up the steps and pushed the door open. It

opened with a loud creak. It wasn't a big house at all.

Actually, it was a shack. Just one big open area. To the

right of the door was an old wooden bed. The mattress was

flat and sunken in with twigs and straws sticking out of it.

There was an old rag or blanket across the mattress. It

looked very uncomfortable. There was a big brick fireplace

in the back of the shack. There was a table to the side of the

fireplace that still had some old, rusted pots and pans on it.

There were two chairs sitting in the middle of the floor in

front of the fireplace. One had a very old dusty-dirty blue

blanket on it.

The inside of the house smelled stale, old, and dusty. Everything was dusty. I walked over to the table, and there was an old doll lying on the floor near it. I picked it up. It was made from black cloth material. It had pieces of tan cloth sewn in for eyes. Brown yarn was used for hair and eyebrows. It wore a green bonnet and a green dress with a floral print on it. There was a brown torn apron tied around the waist of the doll. A feeling of sadness overcame me. If these walls could talk, they would talk about all the sadness, pain, worry, anger, prayers, hopes, and dreams the people who lived here experienced. I took a deep breath and placed the doll on the table sitting up against the pot.

When I looked up to get ready to leave, I noticed that everything looked different. The furniture didn't look as dusty as it did when I walked in, although it still looked uncomfortable. I looked towards the door just as a young woman walked into the room. Shocked, I backed up into the corner near the table. The young woman was pacing

back and forth frantically. She wore a faded, red long-

sleeve dress with a tan apron tied around her waist. Her

long dress stopped just above her ankles, showing her low-

cut boots. Her boots were black; it looked as if they were

made from leather, but the soles of the boots were made of

wood. My feet started hurting just thinking of how

uncomfortable her feet must have been.

The woman continued pacing before she stomped

her foot and screamed out in anger. Then, she turned face

me. She stared directly at me. I knew I needed to apologize

for intruding, but I was too stunned to speak. This woman

looked so familiar, like I had seen her somewhere before.

She looked so young. She couldn't have been no more than

twenty years old. She had beautiful green eyes and light

brown skin. We stared at each other for what seemed like

hours, but I knew it was only for a few seconds. She started

to walk toward me. I took a step back, and my back hit the

wall.

"I'm sorry," I stated.

It seemed like my words went unheard. She walked up to me, reached out, and grabbed the doll I had placed on the table. She stared at the doll for a moment and walked back to the bed and sat down. Just then, another person came in.

"Kitty, what's this I hear bout you planning to run off? Do you know what would happen if Master Edwards heard about this?"

"I don't have a choice," Kitty stated while fondling with the doll in her hand. "Master say he gone sell my baby as soon as it's born. He gone sell my baby to the Pleasant View Plantation. Now, ain't nothin' pleasant about that place Frannie," she continued. "Do you know what they do to young slaves there?" Kitty asked.

Frannie walked over to the chair with the blue blanket on it and pulled it closer to Kitty. I was still standing in the corner of the room with my mouth wide open. They were slaves! I was standing inside of a slave quarter.

"This is not happening!" I whispered to myself.

Frannie was much older than Kitty. Frannie had on a dirty white bonnet, a brown, long-sleeve shirt with flowers printed on it, and a long tan skirt that also stopped just above her ankles. She had on black leather slide-in shoes with a wooden sole. Frannie had salt and pepper curls coming from the side of the bonnet. She had hazel eyes, and her skin was a russet, reddish-brown color. She was a busty round woman. The type of woman you wanted to lay your head on when things were bad. She seemed to have a calming soul. Frannie sat in the chair right across from Kitty and grabbed her hand.

"Now, child, you do have a choice. You just have to make the right one and pray that God will see you through," Franny said. "Now, Master Edwards has a soft spot for you, girl. Master always talking bout them pretty eyes of yours. He's always been protective over you. Why don't you talk to Master? Ask him if you can keep your firstborn."

"He won't!" Kitty stated as she snatched her hand back. "I was there when Mr. Trimble came down from Pleasant View looking for young'ins to purchase. I had to serve that man," she continued.

Kitty stood up and started pacing back and forth again. "Master Edwards told Mr. Trimble I didn't bleed for two months and that I was expecting my first child. Mr. Trimble made an offer, and Master Edwards almost lost his breath, said that was an offer he couldn't refuse. They talked as though I wasn't standing right there! Mr. Trimble wants my baby delivered to him the day it comes into this world. What would that man want with a new baby?" Kitty stopped pacing and looked at Frannie. "I have to run Frannie. It's the only way for me to keep my baby," Kitty said.

Frannie stood up. "Now, you know Master will make an example out of you if you leave and get caught. It ain't gonna be pretty girl! Death would be a privilege compared to the pain you would feel."

"I have to take my chances Fran," Kitty said with tears in her eyes.

"Child, you just married. You can always have more babies."

"No!" Kitty yelled. "I want this baby!" she whispered angrily.

"Where are you going to go?" Frannie asked. "Black Moses don't come to these parts. It's slave states all around us here; you're bound to get caught," Frannie continued in a pleading voice as she sat back down in her chair. "Now, I had to watch your daddy hang, and your mama and brother get sold. You was all but two years old when your family was taken from you. You all I have left, and I don't want to see my grandbaby get hurt. It would just break my heart."

Just then, a loud bell could be heard ringing outside.

"Time to get back to work," Frannie said while getting up from the chair. Frannie looked at Kitty. "Come child," she said with her arms open wide. Kitty stepped to Frannie and embraced her in a hug. Frannie looked at her and wiped some fallen tears from Kitty's eyes.

"You have choices. Just really think before you decide what to do, and I'll pray that God sees you through. Now, I better get back to the field and you better get to the big house before Master come looking for you," Frannie said as she kissed Kitty on her forehead. They both turned to walk out together, closing the door behind them. I was still standing in the corner in disbelief.

"How could they not see me?" I said out loud.

I looked at the doll that was now sitting on the bed. I walked to the door and opened it slowly, afraid of what I might see. I saw nobody, and it was quiet except for the birds, leaves blowing in the wind and the frogs croaking.

I took off running back towards the dirt trail. As I was halfway to the car, I felt that sharp burst of energy again. I stopped running and stumbled against the tree. My arms and legs were tingling again. I took a deep breath, stood up, and started running back to the car. When I finally reached the car, I got in, closed and locked the door, and leaned back against the seat.

I looked over at CeCe; she was still in a deep sleep, her back still turned away from me. Not even my heavy breathing was waking her up. I turned the car on, trying to

leave this area as quickly as possible. I put the car in drive

and glanced at the time. It was 7:05 a.m.

2

Was I dreaming? Did what just happen really happen? I leaned back against my seat, rethinking the conversation that took place between Kitty and Frannie. It all seemed so real. I instantly felt sad. That's a horrible situation for anyone to be in. I looked down at my sneakers; they had mud on them, and there were a few leaves on the floor mat near my feet. The mud was still wet. I shook my head, frustrated and confused.

"I need to get out of here!" I say to myself out loud. I put the car in drive and made a left out of the dirt road onto the two-lane highway going back the way I came. I drove for an hour until I reached the main road. I had never been so happy to see other people. I decided to find a store or gas station that sold phone chargers. When I finally came across a Shell gas station, I noticed a police car behind me. He blocked me in and flashed his red and blue lights when I pulled into a parking space.

"Ugh. What now!" I said to myself. "CeCe!" I yelled while shaking her.

"Wake up and sit your seat back up! We got stopped by the cops. Sit up and put your hands on the dashboard," I said

"What! What happened? What did you do?" she asked while sitting her seat up.

"Nothing," I replied while rolling the windows down and placing my hands on the steering wheel.

"This cannot be happening!" CeCe said nervously.

Just then, the officer approached the window. The officer was wearing a navy-blue, long-sleeve uniform shirt with taupe-colored trousers with a navy-blue stripe on the side of the trousers, and black tactical boots. The typical police uniform. He was Caucasian with short red curly hair. He had a low-cut goatee. I noticed the badge on the left side of his chest and took note of his badge number.

"Good morning," the officer said.

"Good morning. Is there a problem officer?"

"Yes. There is. Hand me your license and registration, and I'm also going to need the ID of that passenger as well."

At this point, I was clearly trying to hide my frustration. I was hoping he would just tell me what the problem was but, clearly, I saw I was going to have to rephrase my question.

"Officer, my license is in my purse. I'm going to remove my left hand from the steering wheel, so I can grab my license and the registration."

"Careful now!" the officer stated with his hand on his hip holster.

"Are there any weapons in the car?" he asked.

"No," I replied.

"Officer. I'm going to use my right hand to get my ID out of my back pocket and the registration in the glove compartment," said CeCe.

"Careful gal! No sudden movements," he warned.

I gave him our ID and the registration and let him know this was a rental car. He snatched the items out of my hand and went to his patrol car. I looked over at CeCe. She had tears in her eyes.

"It's going to be ok," I said.

"How do you know? This man is clearly upset. He basically had his hand on his gun the whole time he was at the window."

"I noticed. Just try to stay calm. We're going to be ok."

"You don't know that!" CeCe yelled.

"I do know if you keep acting like this, you're going to give him a reason to use that gun. Now, calm the hell down!" I yelled, already upset at this situation. I'd never seen CeCe so nervous. She was visibly shaking in her seat, her cheeks wet from the continuous stream of tears falling from her eyes. *Where is all her confidence now?* I wondered to myself.

"What did you do?" she yelled. "Did you run a stop sign or something? Did you hit something? Nobody just pulls you over for nothing!" she yelled quietly.

"Damn it! Would you shut up before you get us both killed! For goodness sakes, CeCe, do you know what state we're in? This is Mississippi! Do you know the history this state holds?" I asked her. "Parts of Mississippi still have sundown towns, where people feel they have the right to kill black people if they're out after dark. Now, stop pissing me off before I kick you out of my car!" I continued.

I loved CeCe. I would never kick her out or leave her. I looked over at CeCe crying. I knew she's just afraid. She knew all about the many black people that had died at the hands of police officers. My heart softened for her. To be honest, I was scared too. But I would never give someone the satisfaction of seeing me scared.

"Look CeCe. I'm sorry for yelling. I would never leave you. You're like the little sister I never wanted," I said jokingly. "Plus, I could never go back to Aunt Gracie's without you. They would kill me themselves." We both let out a little giggle.

"I know you are scared, and I am too. Just try not to show it. I promise I didn't do anything illegal to get pulled over… other than being black," I said.

CeCe wiped the tears from her face. Just then, I noticed the officer getting out of his cruiser and making his way back to us. We placed our hands back on the dashboard.

"Can you tell me what the problem is, officer?" I asked, as he approached the driver's side window.

"Sure... your vehicle was reported missing, and you two ladies fit the description of missing persons as well," the officer stated as he handed me back our IDs and the registration. I exhaled slowly. "You mind telling me what happened?" he asked.

"Sure, we were out doing last-minute shopping. My phone died and we were unable to use our GPS to get back. My cousin and I are not from here."

"I saw, your identification says you're from Arizona, That's a long way from home. What brings y'all to Mississippi?"

"We're here for our family reunion," I answered, slightly irritated. It was really none of his business why we were here. "I was actually going in to buy a charger for my phone."

"Well… you can do that, or I can have you follow me back. I already radioed dispatch to let them know you and Ciera were found," the officer said. "As of right now, y'all about forty minutes out."

I agreed to let the officer lead us back to Aunt Gracie's. When the officer turned around to walk back to the cruiser, I turned to look at CeCe. She looked more relaxed.

"Are you ok?" I asked.

"You know this was my first interaction with an officer. With all the bad things I hear on the news, it's hard to put my trust in them. I really thought that my life was going to end today. All I could really focus on was his hand resting on his gun the whole time he was talking. I'm sorry for the way I was acting and for blaming you."

"You don't have to apologize. I understand where you're coming from. To be honest, I've had many interactions with cops. None of them was good, and none of them was due to me doing anything wrong."

"Really!"

"Yep… and each time, that hand always found its way to the gun."

"Why is it never the taser?" CeCe asked.

"Right! Or the baton. Anything that won't put a bullet through my body."

"You know what's crazy though? Every time a situation like that comes up, I hear Aunt Gracie's voice."

"Brie, I heard it too! Don't tell me!"

We say together, "No weapon formed against me shall prosper." We laughed together, as I started the car and pulled out behind the patrol cruiser.

Forty minutes later, we pull up in front of Aunt Gracie's house. As I pulled into the driveway, the police officer flashed his red and blue lights and sped off. CeCe and I both leaned back into our seats and stared at the house. I didn't know about CeCe but, to me, this was the most beautiful house I'd ever seen at this moment.

It was a colonial-style house with wood panel sidings. It was a white two-story house that sat on a platform. The porch steps connected to a wide porch that wrapped around the front and sides of the house. There was a beautiful bluish-green wood panel door. The blueish-green door matched the shutters placed on the sides of each window. There was one big window on each side of the door. The windows and shutters on the second floor were perfectly aligned with the windows on the first floor. There was also a window right above the front door.

The nearest neighbor was half a mile away. The front yard was big and open. The driveway was a straight shot to the backyard. The backyard was also big and open with tall trees surrounding the property from the front to the back. It could get scary at night. There was no fence surrounding the property, only tall trees.

"You ready?" CeCe asked

"To shower, brush my teeth, and use the toilet... yes. For one hundred and one questions about us getting lost... no," I answered. "Are you ready?" I asked her.

"I guess," she answered while looking out the passenger's side window. "I feel bad we ruined the reunion. We will go down in history for making the family miss the 2022 Taylor Family Reunion," she continued.

My dad started the family reunions. Family meant everything to my father, and he swore to bring us all together every year to celebrate the love, growth, and history of our family. After he died, Aunt Gracie vowed to continue what he started.

"Yeah, me too," I sighed, agreeing with CeCe.

CeCe smacks her lips "Ugh! Now, how am I going to get my phone?"

"Girl bye!" I laughed. "I can't with you. How about you get a J.O.B.?" I laughed as I got out of the car.

"I might have to. Dang, I like my free time," CeCe said as she got out the car.

I noticed Aunt Gracie running out of the front door. "Brielle, Ciera!" she screamed. "Thank God you two are ok," she cried as she ran towards us.

Aunt Gracie was my dad's sister. She looked exactly like my dad, but she had hazel eyes like me. Aunt Gracie was thick in all the right places with an hourglass waistline. She wore her black hair in a pixie cut. She was gorgeous with her golden-brown skin color. Every time I saw Aunt Gracie, a feeling of guilt would creep on me like

31

a snake coming out of nowhere, slithering up my leg and around my waist just to reach my ear and whisper, "It's your fault your daddy is gone."

I thought about that day a lot, but it hurt more every time I looked at my Aunt Gracie. My dad and Aunt Gracie's facial features were identical, except my dad had green eyes and he was about four inches taller than Aunt Gracie. My dad worked out regularly; he was very fit. Auntie Gracie was the baby of the family. She was two years younger than my dad. They were close. Aunt Gracie grabbed CeCe and me and pulled us into a tight hug while she cried.

"We were so worried about you two! Are you alright? What happened? Why didn't y'all call? Are you hurt? You must be tired. Did y'all eat anything? You two must have been so scared? Where did y'all go? Wait! Let's get you cleaned up first. I wanna fix you a plate. Grab your bags and come on in the house," she said as she turned to rush us in the house.

As soon as she turned away, we saw Uncle Mac running toward us. Uncle Mac was Aunt Gracie's husband. He was tall and muscular with dark brown skin. He had a bald head with a neatly trimmed beard. He had an easy-going personality, yet was always the life of the party.

"Girls!" he yelled as he pulled us into a tight hug, giving us both a forehead kiss. "Thank God y'all ok! We been out searchin' for y'all all night. What happened? Where did y'all—"

"Malcolm, let them girls come in the house and settle down before you start with your nonstop questions!" He was cut off by Aunt Gracie before she disappeared into the house. CeCe and I laughed.

"Dang Uncle Mac! She was knocking us out with those questions. I couldn't breathe," I said, laughing.

"That was an all-time record. What was that, like twenty questions in 10 seconds?" CeCe asked, laughing.

"I told you I wasn't ready," I told CeCe.

"You know how your aunt is," Uncle Mac said, laughing with us.

"Uh, Uncle Mac, that's wrong. How you throw Aunt Gracie out there like you wasn't getting started? You just as bad as she is," I said, laughing.

"Right! You would have still been questioning us had Aunty Gracie not stopped you," said CeCe. We all laughed.

"Well, if we didn't love you, we wouldn't care now, would we?" he said, slightly embarrassed. "Now, gimmie them bags," Uncle Mac said while holding out his hands. "Let's get y'all inside," he said with a big smile on his face.

Once inside, I ran straight to the guest room I was

staying in. Thankfully, it had an attached bathroom. After finally relieving myself, I took a shower, brushed my teeth, and got dressed for the day. It was barely eleven-thirty a.m. it and was already hot outside. I could tell it was going to be a hot day. I threw on a pink and white spaghetti strap sundress and white sandals and put my braids in a ponytail.

I fell back onto the bed and took a deep breath. The bed was so comfortable. I wouldn't mind taking a thirty-minute nap. I looked around the room. The room was nicely decorated. The walls around the house were a bluish-green color with white crown molding and floor trim throughout the house. The guest room had a queen size canopy bed with a grey comforter and grey pillows all over the bed. The canopy was draped in white sheer fabric. They had long gray curtains that barely touched the floor.

There were two nightstands on both sides of the bed. Near the corner of the room, there was a thin full-length mirror. When you pushed a small button on the side of it, it opened to a hidden shelf that held bath towels, blankets, and pillows for the guests. There was a six-drawer dresser that had a fifty inch flat-screen tv mounted to the wall above it. There was an archway that led to the bathroom. To the right was a vanity with a cushy stool underneath the table. To the left was a walk-in closet. Straight to the back of the bathroom was a step-down jet tub with a shower. To the left of that was a door that led to the toilet. The bathroom and rooms had a light-gray plush carpet.

Uncle Mac was a contractor. He and Aunt Gracie were almost done renovating the house. From the looks of the outside of the house, you would never guess how updated and beautiful the inside was. Just outside the archway on the wall was a floating shelf. There was a candle, a succulent plant and a picture frame of Aunt Gracie and her two brothers, my dad and Uncle Glen. Uncle Glen was CeCe's dad.

I stared at the picture while lying down. I missed my dad. I still couldn't believe he was gone. My dad's name was Gerald Tayler. He always wore his curly hair cut short: a fade on the sides and curls on the top. My dad died three years ago. It was the day I turned eighteen. The worst day of my life, the day my life became incomplete. It was also the day I stopped praying.

It was that time of the month. I had come back from the store an hour prior with some much-needed items. One of those items was a box of tampons that I couldn't find. I got upset and figured I must have left the box on the counter at the store. I was getting ready to go back to the store with the receipt, but my dad stopped me and offered to go for me. Not even two minutes after he left, I heard tires screeching and a loud bang. I ran outside. Nothing could have prepared me for what I was about to see. My dad made it to the light. His car was in the middle of the intersection where a semi-truck struck the driver side of the car. The truck driver T-boned my dad's car; his car spun around and came to stop with the front of his car facing the semi-truck.

All I heard besides me screaming was a loud horn sound coming from his car. The whole driver's side of the car was smashed in. I knew in my heart he didn't survive, but that didn't stop me from trying to get to him. I was almost to him when someone grabbed me and pulled me back to the curb. I tried to fight them, but the person held a tight grip on my arm and pulled me into an embrace. I turned around to see my mom.

"You don't need to see that baby," she said as she's going hysterical herself. I just squeezed her tightly, as both of us felt like a part of our soul was just ripped away from us.

Three days later, I was sitting on the floor in my walk-in closet, cleaning up after looking for pictures and what did I see? A box of tampons! It was the box I thought I had left at the store. I just stared at the box while a steady stream of tears fell down my face.

"Mom!" I yelled.

"Yea! is everything all right?" she asked as she approached my closet.

"No," I responded while holding up the box of tampons. Her face went blank. "It's my fault daddy is gone!" I cried. "I didn't leave it at the store. It was in my closet the whole time!" I screamed.

My mom dropped to her knees and held me while we cried together. I blamed myself for my dad's death. Deep down, I think my mom blamed me too. Shortly after my dad's funeral, my mom quit her job as a marriage therapist and became a flight attendant. She said she needed a break from listening to other people's marriage problems while she was grieving the loss of hers. Honestly, I think she became a flight attendant to get away from me.

My thoughts were interrupted by a knock at the door. I wiped the tears from my face and sat up on the bed. "Come in!"

"You ok?" CeCe asked.

"Yeah, just relaxing a bit."

"Well, Aunt Gracie said to come eat; your plate is getting cold."

CeCe changed into a red two-piece crop top with a matching skirt. The skirt was long with two splits on the side. She wore her long wavy hair down.

"Well, let's go eat!" I said as I got up from the bed.

The day just seemed to fly by. Aunt Gracie and Uncle Mac called the family to let them know CeCe and I made it back safely. One by one, people started to trickle in. The next thing I knew, there were just over one hundred people partying in the backyard. Every chair and table CeCe and I set up was just about being used.

The family reunion went on as planned since there was an even bigger cause for a celebration. There were lots of games being played, food being eaten, dancing, hugs, and, of course, questions about CeCe and I getting lost. I caught a glimpse of CeCe walking around with a decorative cup in her hand, asking for donations for a new phone. I shook my head. *That girl,* I thought to myself, as I sat at the table taking in the scenery.

As the evening rolled in, Aunt Gracie hooked up the microphone to the speaker and got everyone's attention. "Ugh um," she cleared her throat. "Can everyone hear me?"

"Yeah!"

"You good Gracie!"

"Yep, we can hear you!" everyone said in unison.

"Good! Um… CeCe, can you bring me the brown box on the dining room table please?" Aunt Gracie, continued as CeCe disappeared into the house.

"Ok family, it's really a blessing that we are all here today for our 5th annual Taylor family reunion. I don't know about you, but it feels so good when you don't have to get reintroduced to your family every five years. It's a blessing to see how much this family has grown since the 1st family reunion."

CeCe reappeared with a big box in her hand. She sat it on the table near Aunt Gracie.

"Thank you, baby!" Aunt Gracie said. She continued speaking, "As some of you may know, it was my brother Gerald who started this annual reunion. It was his personal goal to see that this family continues to grow and flourish. After he died, it became my personal goal. I want to thank everyone that traveled near and far for being here today. I know that some of you have flights to catch tonight and some of you tomorrow morning, so I'm going to make this quick." Aunt Gracie opened the box, pulled out a thin booklet and held it up.

"Before you leave here today, please make sure to grab a booklet. I was able to update the family tree. I was also able to add some old obituaries and newspaper articles on our family members. There are pictures and some very fascinating information I stumbled across about the Taylor family and where we come from. It took a lot for me to put this together, so please don't forget to grab one. Again, I want to thank everyone for coming out to our 5th Annual Taylor Family Reunion. Have a safe trip back, and I do expect phone calls or text messages to let me know you made it back safely."

Aunt Gracie ended the night with a prayer, "Heavenly Father, we come to you with gratefulness on our hearts. We thank you for allowing us to come together and celebrate another year with this beautiful family that you have blessed us with. We thank you for watching over Ciera and Brielle and bringing them back to us safely, Lord. Lord, we ask that you forgive us for our transgressions whether it's something we've done deliberately or unintentionally. We ask that you watch over and protect us on our journey back home. Keep us safe from any danger seen and unseen. We pray that you protect us and guide us both now and forevermore. In Jesus' name, Amen!"

"Amen," everyone said in unison.

One by one, slowly but surely, everyone started to leave, giving out goodbye hugs and kisses and grabbing a booklet. Uncle Mac hopped on the mic.

"Please make sure to grab a plate on your way out. There is plenty of food leftover y'all," he said.

I helped Uncle Mac and Aunt Gracie put the table and chairs away in the backyard. They ended up having a party of their own, so I went in the house to see if CeCe needed help cleaning and putting away the food.

"Hey girl, how you doing in here? You need any help?"

"Um... yeah, I could use some help. I'm almost done in here. The only things left to do is to wipe down the countertops and sweep up," she said as she put the last bit of dishes in the dishwasher.

"Ok, I'll clean the countertops," I stated as I reached under the sink for the spray and a clean towel. The kitchen was big and open with a formal eat-in dining room. There was an island in the middle of the kitchen. There were four bar stools at the island. The counter space wrapped around the backend of the kitchen. There was a wide window at the kitchen sink, a double oven near the

45

stove. There was a lot of cabinet space. The cabinets were white with light gray marble countertops.

"So, how did you do on your donations?" I asked.

"Actually... I did way better than expected. Girl, I ended up with $650."

"Stop playing!" I said, smacking my lips.

"Seriously! I did, and I didn't even come to you for a donation," she laughed.

"Wow, our family really came through," I said.

"Yeah, but I think they were more generous because of us being lost. Everyone was really concerned," CeCe said.

"I know. Do Uncle Glen know what happened to us?" I asked. He couldn't take time off work, so he missed this year's reunion.

"Yea, Aunt Gracie and Uncle Mac keep him updated. Do your mom know we were missing?" CeCe asked.

"No, I'm sure she's on a plane somewhere. I'll update her when I get home. She is supposed to arrive home tomorrow morning."

"What time does our plane leave tomorrow?" CeCe asked.

"At eleven a.m.," I answered.

"Well. I'm about to turn in. I am beat," CeCe said, yawning as she finished sweeping the floor.

"I'm right behind you," I said as I put the towel away. I glanced out the window and smiled. "I don't know how we gone get any sleep though. Uncle Mac and Aunt Gracie still partying. Girl, look at her! Now, she knows she does not need to be dropping it like that," I said while laughing. CeCe made her way to the window.

"She gone be in pain tomorrow. Look at them knees shaking." We both laughed, as I turned away and grabbed a booklet off the table.

"Well, goodnight," I said as I walked towards my room.

"Night!" replied CeCe while still staring out the window with a smile on her face.

I took a quick shower and brushed my teeth. I leaned back on the bed and glanced at the time. Eleven-forty-five p.m. Aunt Gracie and Uncle Mac were still partying by themselves. I picked up the booklet and started skimming through it.

Man. Aunt Gracie went all out with her research, I thought to myself as I flipped through the obituary section and found my dad's. I read over it and turned the page. I read over some cousins' and great's obituaries, some of whom I was familiar with. The newspaper articles talked about some accomplishments and events that honored some of my relatives. Towards the end of the booklet was a big family tree. I started with my name, then my dad's, and worked my way up to the top. My mouth dropped open.

"Oh, my God!" I said aloud as I sat up in the bed. I saw Frannie Taylor listed as my 5th great-grandmother with the dates 1814-1902. She had one son, Joe Taylor. I flashed back to when Frannie said, "I had to watch my son hang."

Oh, my God! That was my 4th great-grandfather. Joe married a woman named Martha and had two children, Kitty and Boe. Kitty was my 3rd great-grandmother, 1845-1932. I thought back to the conversation between the Frannie and Kitty.

"It was real! It wasn't a dream," I said aloud.

I could never tell anyone about this. How would I

explain it? How did this even happen? Why did it happen? I continued to look through the booklet. At the end of the book was a letter from Aunt Gracie explaining the story she found about Kitty, or should I say grandma Kitty.

I started this journey for myself but, in the midst of me trying to find out where I or we come from, I came across some documentation from the state archives. I was unable to take pictures, print or copy anything, but I was able to read and learn about our great-grandma Kitty. Kitty was a very strong woman. I learned that Kitty was a house slave for the Oak Lake Manor Plantation. Kitty fell in love and was granted permission to marry at 15 years old. At age 17, Kitty found out she was pregnant with her first baby. Master Edwards had planned to sell Kitty's baby to the Pleasant View Plantation. This plantation had a reputation for torturing and overworking slave kids. Kitty refused to let her baby be sold and made the choice to run away. The only family she left behind was Fannie. Joe

Taylor, her father was hung and Kitty's mom and brother were sold. I wasn't able to find any information on them. Kitty made the hard choice to leave her husband and her grandma Frannie. I found old wanted flyers for Kitty. She must have been special to the slave owner because he spent months looking for her.

While on the run, Kitty befriended a white woman named Sue, who thankfully didn't agree with slavery. It just so happened she was pregnant also. Sue and her husband allowed Kitty to stay in a secret room underneath their house. Kitty helped out with chores and, in return, Sue would teach Kitty how to read and write. Sue helped deliver Kitty's babies! That's right y'all, Kitty had twin boys. Isn't God good? Can you imagine the hardship and worry Kitty faced and the bravery to leave her grandmother and husband while pregnant. Not long after slavery ended, Sue and her family moved to another state and left Kitty their house.

I'm so grateful I stumbled upon this information. We can learn a lot from Grandma Kitty. She put her faith in God and was showered with blessings. If it wasn't for Kitty's determination, we would not be here today!

I didn't realize I was holding my breath until I finished reading the letter. I didn't get it. Why did I see what I saw? Why is all this information being given to me now? I had so many questions but the one I want answered the most is, why is this happening to me?

3

The flight home was quick, at least for me it was. I was busy trying to figure out how I was able to see Kitty and Franny and why. When we reached the airport back home in Phoenix, Arizona, we instantly found Ciera's mom, Sherri. She was very easy to spot. Her long black hair was braided back in cornrows. And, of course, her edges were laid as well. Sherri and CeCe were like sisters. Their styles were almost the same. Just like CeCe, her mom stayed camera ready too.

"Hey girls! How was your flight" she asked as she hugged and kissed CeCe.

"Horrible! This man I sat next to was eating the whole flight, just smacking in my ear. Then slurped every time he took a drink. I wanted to throw up. Then, his kid was no better. She would dig in her nose and try to write on the window with her snot."

"Ewe," Sherri said as she scrunched up her face.

"I know mom. Next time, I'm flying first class."

"As long as you have first-class money honey," Aunt Sherri said as she patted CeCe on her back.

CeCe rolled her eyes and mumbled something under her breath. "It's not like we can't afford it."

"We? Let me correct you. I can afford first-class. You can't," Aunt Sherri replied. Aunt Sherri turned to me. "How was your flight, Brie?" she asked as she hugged and kissed me.

"It was good, I was lucky to get a row to myself."

"Yeah. Near the emergency exit," CeCe said, smacking her lips.

"Don't hate. I told you to book early with me. When I booked, most of the seats on the plane were still available."

Sherri turned to CeCe. "Looks like procrastination has caused you to miss out yet again, isn't that right Ciera?"

"Ugh, mom! I don't feel like talking about this right now! Can we just go home please?" CeCe said, clearly frustrated and rolling her eyes.

"Girl, you want to try again with that tone? Don't get beat!"

"Mama, I'm twenty-one! I'm grown, you can't whip me." CeCe smirked.

"You may be too old for the belt, but you aren't too old to catch these hands!" Aunt Sherri took a step towards CeCe, her voice stern and slightly louder. "What you don't seem to understand Ciera is that you may be twenty-one, but you act like your sixteen so, since you want to act like a child, that puts me well into my parental rights to tear that ass up. Now, I'm going to ask you again. You want to try again with that tone?"

"Mom, this is embarrassing."

"No. You're embarrassing! I'm done raising you. Grow up and get a job!"

"I don't want to work while I'm in school."

"Girl, you take one class twice a week! I don't want to hear it."

"Aunt Sherri," I said, trying to break up the argument. "Is it ok if we grab a bite to eat before you drop me off?"

"Sure," she answered while still glaring at CeCe.

I honestly didn't know what CeCe was afraid of when it came to responsibility. I loved the freedom of making my own choices, coming and going as I pleased. I worked part-time and went to school full-time. The only thing left was for me to move out, but my mom worked so much that I practically had the house to myself. I loved adulting.

Just as we were making our way to the exit door, I hear somebody yell, "Brielle!" I turned and looked through the crowds and found my mom coming down the escalator, waving at me.

"Mama!" I said, shocked to see her. I turned to Aunt Sherri. "I thought she would have been home already. Her flight was supposed to arrive at five a.m."

"Maybe something happened with her flight," she replied, shrugging her shoulders.

"Hey ladies!" my mom said as she approached us. She hugged each of us with a big smile on her face.

I didn't know how much I missed my mom until now. She wore her natural hair in loose curls. My mother was beautiful in her navy-blue flight attendant uniform. She was a very curvaceous woman, but she wasn't always like that. Before my dad died, we could wear each other's clothes. While mourning my dad, she put on some extra pounds, but it looked good on her.

"Hey, Brenda!" Aunt Sherri hugged her back.

"I'm so glad I spotted you guys! Sherri, do you mind if I tag along with you guys? I don't have a ride."

"Sure, we were going to grab a bite to eat first before swinging by your place."

"Perfect! I'm starving."

"Mom, I thought you would have been home already; you said your flight was supposed to get here at five this morning."

"It was. But we got delayed for a while. A fight broke out between a few drunk passengers. Oh! I'm sorry, I want you guys to meet my friend Donnie. Donnie, this is my daughter Brielle."

He extended out his hand to me. Donnie had to be at least six foot-three. I literally had to look up at him. But, then again, everyone was taller than me except for CeCe. His hair was black and styled in short dreadlocks; the sides of his hair was in a fade, and he had a thin goatee. His skin was an amber, deep dark brown color. He was also wearing a navy-blue flight attendant uniform. He held out his hand to shake my hand, and I took his hand. His hands were huge, completely covering my hand.

"Nice to meet you!" he said, squeezing my hand a little too tightly.

"This is my sister-in-law Sherri and her daughter Ciera"

"Wow! I could have bet money you two were sisters. Nice to meet you," he said, shaking Sherri and CeCe's hands.

59

"Nice to meet you as well," said Aunt Sherri. CeCe just gave him a little smirk. Donnie turned to my mom, handing her the luggage.

"Well, Brenda. Since you found a ride home, I'm going to head out."

"Ok. Thanks for your help!" my mom said as she hugged Donnie. My mom wasn't as short as me. She was 5'10. Her arms easily wrapped around Donnie's neck.

"No problem, talk to you later." He looked at us before turning to leave. "Nice to meet y'all again," he said as he waved goodbye.

*****

I woke up to the sound of the doorbell. I looked at the clock on my nightstand, and it was six twenty-three p.m. I'd been asleep for six hours. I really hoped whoever was on the other side of that door went away. This bed was too comfortable for me to move.

I look around my room, thankful that I cleaned it before I left for Mississippi. I loved my room. I had my white queen size bed with a purple and black comforter and purple and black pillows all over it. I had a white desk in the corner. There was a purple fluffy rug in the middle of the floor. I loved fluffy rugs. I even had a fluffy rug in my walk-in closet. I had a white dresser with a mirror against the wall next to my closet. I'd been meaning to switch my furniture around. My mirror was facing my bedroom window. If my purple curtains were open, the glare from the sun brightened up my room too much.

What I loved most about my room was the big chocolate cupcake decal on my wall. It was a gift from my dad the morning of my eighteenth birthday. When I opened my eyes that morning, the first thing I saw were the words 'still my' and a big chocolate cupcake with white icing and purple and pink sprinkles. He meant it as a joke, but I loved it. That was his nickname for me, Cupcake. The doorbell rang again.

"Brie, can you get the door please?" my mom yelled from her room. Sounded like she was sleeping too.

"Yeah," I grunted, not wanting to get up. I walked down the hall looking at the many pictures on the wall of my family, back when we were happy and complete.

I could tell my mom was trying to move on. She had grieved the loss of my dad for a long time, but I wouldn't say she had healed from his loss until she returned to her career as a marriage therapist. I missed having her around.

I slowed down when I got to the living room, noticing that everything was still the same since when my dad was around. I could see him sitting on his favorite navy-blue reclining chair watching his favorite movie, *Die Hard*. His chair sat in the corner of the room; there was a gray sectional with a chaise that sat across from the chair. A small white side table sat next to the chair with a silver lamp on top. The white coffee table sat in the middle of the floor. There was also a light blue, gray and white area rug that covered a part of the living room floor. Gray hard wood floor flowed throughout the house. The flat screen tv hung on the wall above the fireplace. The doorbell rang again.

"I'm coming!" I yelled, slightly frustrated. I opened the door to CeCe holding a box of pizza and a duffle bag hanging from her shoulder. She had on blue jeans and a white crop top, her hair in a curly ponytail.

"What took you so long?" she asked as she barged her way in, walking towards the kitchen.

"We were sleep. Why didn't you call before you decided to come over?" I asked as I closed the door.

"I don't have a phone. Remember?"

"Oh. That's right. You broke it," I said with a smirk.

"Brie. Who's at the door?" Mama asked.

"Ciera," I answered.

"Oh, ok."

"Hi Aunty Brenda."

"Hey CeCe," my mom replied, as we walked down the hall to my room.

CeCe dropped her bag on my floor, closed the door and fell back on the bed. "Ugh," she sighed.

"Um... what's the bag for?" I asked while grabbing a pillow and sitting on the floor.

"I'm going to a slumber party."

"Aren't you a little old for a slumber party?" I laughed. CeCe lifted her head up to look at me.

"Are you?"

"Uh… yeah. Who's having a slumber party?"

"You are," CeCe laughed.

"Uh, negative! I just plan on slumbering. Ain't no party here. Didn't you get enough of me in Mississippi?"

"I just had to get out of the house. My mom has been tripping since the airport. She even tried to take my car."

"Tried! How did you get out of that one?"

"My dad talked her out of it. Said he wasn't about to drive me around or give me money for Uber."

"Well CeCe… what are you so afraid of? Don't you want to me more independent?"

CeCe closed her eyes and took a deep breath. She got up and sat on the floor facing me, leaning back against the bed.

"I feel like being an adult is too stressful, too complicated. What if I make the wrong decisions and something goes wrong? I like the way things are right now. My parents know what's best for me. I feel safer when they make choices for me."

I look at CeCe with a shocked look on my face. "You're kidding, right?"

"No! See, that's why I don't open-up to people. Everyone keeps asking me what I'm afraid of. You're the only person I'm honest with, and you judge me and make fun." CeCe got up, frustrated.

"I'm not judging you. Am I shocked at your answer? Yes. But you can't help the way you feel. Do you want my advice?"

"Yeah," CeCe said as she looked down at the carpet

while her fingers played with the fibers.

"Grow up!" I yelled as I threw a pillow at her, hitting her in her head.

"Ugh really!" she yelled out of frustration while throwing the pillow back at me. I dodged it and it hit the wall. I laughed.

"I'm just playing! Listen. Your parents knew what was best for you when you were a child. Now that you are an adult, it's time for you to figure out what's best for you. Write out some goals for yourself. Then, plan how you will reach them."

"Like what type of goals? Marriage, kids… I've already done that."

"Well, those are goals, but they don't help better yourself. What about a career goal? What type of career do you want?" I asked.

"I don't know. There are so many jobs out there, I—"

"No," I cut her off. "Not a job, a career. What do you love to do? What's your passion? What makes you happy?"

"I never thought about it like that. I love working out. I like how it makes me feel."

"Ok. So, you could be a personal trainer, dietitian, physical therapist."

CeCe smiled. "That sounds fun! Getting paid for doing what I love!"

"Yeah. That's called a career."

"I also love throwing parties!"

"Ok. You could also be a coordinator! You could plan a wedding and get the bride in shape at the same time. That would be a cool business."

"Wow! I'm really getting excited. That sounds fun!"

I laughed while looking a CeCe. She was looking up at the ceiling. It was like a light bulb turned on in her head. I could see her getting motivated.

"Now, if you want to reach your career goal faster, enroll in more than one class. Go full-time. Talk to a counselor. They'll tell you the classes you need to take. Your parents never had the job versus career talk with you?"

"No! It was always hurry up and get a job, you need a job, grow up," CeCe said while rolling her eyes.

"Well, get one."

"One what?"

"A job, it's nothing like having your own money. You could work part time and go to school full time like me. Plus, it would get Aunt Sherri off your back."

"What kind of life would I have without her nagging me? That's how we spend most of our days."

I laid down on the floor and turned to look at the cupcake on my wall. "My dad and I use to have these types of talks all the time."

"What are you going to school for?"

"I want to be a therapist like my mama. I'm just not sure what type of therapist."

"Do you think things would be different if your dad was still around?"

"Um…. Not really. I probably wouldn't be by myself at home all the time. I'm sure mama would have kept her career as a marriage therapist. You know I can understand about you stressing on making the right decisions. Ever since the day my dad died, I stress over the little decisions. Simple day to day things like if I cook, I could risk setting the house on fire or, if I order food, the delivery driver may spit in my food. Ew. Or worst, taste it."

"That's a bit extreme, don't you think?" CeCe asked.

"Yeah. But that's how I feel. As if any and every decision I make can and will have a negative outcome. I regretted offering to do that last-minute supply run for the family reunion. You saw how that turned out. We could have lost our life that day."

"Yeah. But we didn't," CeCe said as she crawled over to me. She laid next to me on the floor. "Do you feel like you had a choice the day your dad died?"

"Yeah... if only I had decided to look for the stupid box of tampons instead of getting upset and assuming the cashier didn't bag it, my dad would still be here."

"Have you talked to anybody about how you feel?"

"Who would I talk to?" I said as I turned to look at CeCe and tried to stop the tears that were about to fall from my eyes. "I already feel like it's my fault he's gone. Whenever the family looks at me, I feel like they are blaming me too. I mean, come on CeCe. My mom changed her career after I told her I found the box of tampons and, of all things, a flight attendant! Just the job to take when you don't want to be around someone."

"Aww, that's not true Brie! I don't blame you."

"Well thanks, but it doesn't help the way I feel," I said while wiping the tears that escaped.

"Do you want my advice?"

"Yeah, I guess."

"It sounds to me like the future therapist needs a therapist," CeCe said, giving me a soft smile.

72

"Right! Anyway," I said as I sat up, ready to change the subject. "Did you read the booklet Aunt Gracie made?"

"Yeah. About our newfound greats? Yeah, I read it."

"What if I told you I saw them."

"Saw who?" CeCe asked, looking confused.

"Grandma Kitty and Grandma Frannie. What if I told you I knew the situation she was in before I read the booklet."

CeCe sat up and leaned against the bed. "So, you telling me you saw our dead great grandparents? What... did they come to you in a dream and introduce themselves?" CeCe asked with a blank look on her face.

"No, I honestly didn't know they were relatives until I saw them in the booklet."

"When did this happen?"

"That morning we slept in the car. I got out to use the bathroom. Do you remember me waking you up that morning?"

"No. Only to tell me the police was pulling us over."

"Well. I was walking through the woods and saw an abandoned shack. For some reason, I went inside."

"For what? To use the bathroom?" she asked.

"No. I guess I was just being nosey. Anyway, I walked in to look around and Kitty stormed in upset. Frannie came in soon after. They were talking but didn't see me." CeCe just stared at me. Her expression was unreadable. I couldn't tell if she believed me or not.

"It was you!" she shouted.

"Huh?"

"You were the one that had the imaginary friend.

74

What was it? Apple! Her name was Apple," she said, laughing.

"She was not imaginary. She was real!" I was getting annoyed.

"Brielle! No parent is going to name their child Apple!"

"Her name was Applonia. We called her Apple for short."

"Who's we? I have never seen her," she laughed.

"It's not my fault she always left right before you came over. I wonder what happened to her. I'll never forget about her and her pink hair," I said with a smile at the memory.

"Pink hair! Really? Do you hear yourself?" CeCe laughed. "You've always been a dreamer."

"She was real!"

"Yeah okay... I'm going to go grab a slice. You want some?" CeCe asked, getting up.

"Yeah. I'll put on a movie," I said, as CeCe walked out of the room still laughing. I was really hoping she would have believed me about Kitty and Frannie. Honestly, I wouldn't believe it either.

"I guess this is just something I have to keep to myself," I say out loud to myself as I search for a movie.

"Ooh! Love and Basketball. Let's watch that!" CeCe said, startling me.

"Aww. Let's watch something funny." I whined.

"I had enough laughs talking about Apple."

I threw a pillow at her head. She ducked out the way while holding two plates with pizza.

"If you make me drop it, you're eating it!" she said while handing me my plate. "I like Love and Basketball.

76

It's one of my favorite movies."

"Fine," I said, giving in.

"You want to come with me to get my phone tomorrow?"

"No. I want to spend the day with my mom tomorrow. I haven't seen her in two weeks. We have a lot of catching up to do. Plus, I still have to tell her about us getting lost in Mississippi. It'll be nice to have a girl's day out. Maybe do some shopping, get our nails done. Maybe catch a movie."

"Sounds fun. I'm trying to get away from my mom and you're trying to bond with yours. We're never on the same page," CeCe said while rolling her eyes and taking a bite of her pizza.

The next morning, I woke up on the floor with a pillow and a blanket. I noticed the covers on my bed were undone and instantly got upset. I know this girl did not have me sleep on the floor while she slept in my bed.

"Ciera!" I yelled as I sat up. The bed was empty. I look at the clock; it was 10:26. "Ugh. I hate waking up late," I said to myself. I smelled bacon cooking, so I went into the kitchen, shocked to see my mom making breakfast.

"Morning!" she said with a smile.

"Hey, I thought you were CeCe."

"Oh. Sorry to disappoint," she laughed "She left about forty-five minutes ago."

"Ugh!... I'm going to beat her. She could have at least made my bed up."

"It's good to see you two are still so close."

"She is the closest thing I have to a sister," I said as I stole a piece of bacon while her back was turned.

78

"I saw that!" she said with her back still turned.

"Impossible! How?" I laughed.

"A good parent never reveals their secrets."

I shook my head. She'd been giving me that same answer since I was little. I didn't even know why I still asked.

"When do you go back to work?" she asked with her back still turned to me.

"Tomorrow. When do you go back?"

"In two weeks, I'm taking some time off to unwind."

"Hey mom. Let's have a girl's day. Do some shopping, get our nails done. It's been a long time since we hung out."

"Yeah. That sounds like fun!"

"We haven't talked in like two weeks. There's a lot to catch up on."

"Yeah. Like you and Ciera getting lost in Mississippi," she said, turning to me to hand me a plate of French toast, bacon and eggs. She took a seat next to me at the island. My mouth dropped open.

"Who told you?"

"Gracie called me last night to make sure you and Ciera made it home safely. Apparently, you forgot to call her."

"Oh," I said as I stuffed my mouth with French toast. I missed my mom's cooking. Her French toast was one of my favorites. Not only was the flavor popping, but the best part was the caramelized sugar she sprinkled on the toast. It was heaven in my mouth.

"I fell asleep."

"Yeah. She figured that much. Were you going to tell me?" she asked between bites.

"Yeah. Today," I replied as I reached over to grab the orange juice that was already sitting on the counter. I poured us a glass. We talked about my trip to Mississippi and her encounter with entitled passengers. I kept my experience with Frannie and Kitty to myself.

After breakfast, mom went to her room to get dressed, and I cleaned the kitchen. On the way to my room to get dressed for the day, mom yelled, "Brie, Donnie is going to hang out with us today."

"Ugh... really mom?" I asked as I entered her room. She was standing in the mirror pulling up some white skinny jeans. Her natural curls bouncing as she jumped into her jeans.

"Yeah, it will be fun."

"No, it won't. It's supposed to be a girl's day out. Men don't like shopping and getting their nails done."

"Some men do," she said as she put on a black button-down halter top.

"Mom, I haven't seen you in two weeks. I wanted you to myself today. I don't even know him. This is not part of the plan," I said, irritated.

"Well, plans change Brielle. Now, go get dressed; he'll be here any minute."

I went in my room, closed the door and laid back on my bed. I didn't even want to go anywhere with her now. I should've gone with CeCe. Just then, my phone rang. I answered it without looking at the caller ID.

"Hello," I answered dryly.

"Hey Brielle, this is Ami. I'm sorry to bother you. I

know you are still out on vacation, but is there any possible way you can come in today? We had three call-ins, and we are short-staffed. Listen, before you answer, I'll extend your vacation day by one day."

"Yea, I'm free," I answered without a second thought.

"Yea! You're the best. I'm buying you lunch. How soon can you get here?"

"Um, I can be there in fifteen to twenty minutes."

"Ok perfect, see you then!"

"Ok, thanks!"

"No, thank you!" Ami said before disconnecting the line. I got up to get dressed. I worked at Ami's boutique. We didn't really have uniforms, but the sales associates had to wear black shoes, black pants and either a black or white shirt. I quickly put on my black pants and white blouse, thankful that I wouldn't have to go out with mom and Donnie.

After putting half my braids into a bun and leaving the back down, I did my edges, grabbed my purse and keys, and opened the door. The moment I stepped into the hallway, my mom came out of her room. She looked at me with a frown on her face.

"Why are you dressed like you're going to work?"

"I am going to work," I answered with a smile on my face.

"But you just told me you go back to work tomorrow!"

"Ami called, said they were short staff—"

"And you conveniently offered to come in," she said, cutting me off.

"Well, like you said mom. Plans change," I said,

using her own words against her. I couldn't help but to smile.

"No! You're not going to work Brielle! We have plans. Call Ami back and..."

She was cut off by the sound of her phone ringing. She ran to the phone and yelled out, "Don't you go nowhere! I'm not through with you!"

I took the time to make a run for it. As soon as I opened the door, Donnie was standing there with a big smile on his face "Hey, it's Brielle, right?"

I frowned at him, instantly annoyed at how he said my name. "Mom. your friend is here!" I yelled.

"Wait Brie!" she yelled back from her room.

"Bye, mom!"

I walked out the door past Donnie. He grabbed my arm squeezing tightly, yanking me towards him. "Where do you think you're going?" he asked. His smile was gone. His face now had a frown, and his eyes were dark with anger. I could have sworn his voice changed. I was unsure if he was angry because I wasn't going with them or because I was walking out on my mom. Either way, it was none of his business. I snatched my arm back.

"Don't ever touch me, and where I'm going is no business of yours!" I said as I start walking to my pearl-white Nissan Maxima parked in front of the house. I started the car and rolled the windows down. I couldn't believe how hot it was already and it was just after eleven o'clock in the morning.

Just before I pulled away, I heard Donnie yell out, "Bye Brielle!" with a big smile on his face.

I was instantly filled with dread. Something was off with Donnie. Should I have not gone to work? Should I have stayed and gotten to know Donnie? Or did I just unleash the devil's spawn?

4

I must have been on autopilot. I didn't even remember the drive to work. All I could focus on was the bad vibes I got when I thought about Donnie. I was starting to regret my decision to go to work. I hated the thought of leaving my mom alone with that man. For a moment, I considered calling Ami and tell her something came up and that I actually couldn't work today. But since I had already committed, that might cost me my job. After realizing that my mom and Donnie had probably already left from the house and that I didn't know where they were going, I decided to just stay at work. I had the urge to say a quick prayer for my mom's safety, then decided against it. God didn't answer my prayers. If he did, my dad would still be here.

When I walked into Ami's Boutique, I head straight to the back to the break room to put my bag in the locker and clock in. I walked back onto the sales floor and saw

Ami behind the cash register on her phone. She looked upset. There were a few customers shopping. I walked up to the counter.

"Hey Ami!"

"Hey Brielle" she said without looking up. Ami was the owner and manager of the boutique. Every other week, Ami's hair was a different color. This week was purple. Her purple and black locs were styled in a Mohawk. She wore a sleeveless, fitted summer dress that had pink, purple, and blue paint splattered on it and black flats. She had a diamond stud nose piercing. Ami was also a fashion designer. Just about half of the clothes in the boutique were clothes she designed.

"Everything ok?" I asked. Ami's eyes were glued to her cell phone.

"No." She showed me her phone. "I need to find some new employees ASAP!"

I saw Adrian, Erica and Kim posting live videos of themselves at a waterpark. My eyes grew big. "Oh, my goodness! Did they just post this?"

"Yep. All three of them are supposed to be home with food poisoning. I knew something was up when all three called in within one minute of each other."

"How long have you known they were at the waterpark?"

"I only just seen the videos when you walked in. I can't wait to put this in their faces."

I shook my head in disbelief. "Wow, social media can really get you caught up."

"Yep. Be careful what you post. In the meantime, you know anybody that needs a job?"

"As a matter of fact, I do! My cousin, Ciera."

"Can you vouch for her?"

"Yeah, she's dependable, she loves fashion; honestly, she would love working here."

"Good! Then, the job is hers if she wants it. Have her come down to fill out an application and to have a little chat with me. I'll fill her in on the job details."

"I will. Thanks, Ami."

"No problem. I wanted to start training you for a manager position. I'm about to open my second store and I won't be here as much."

"Really? Congrats!"

"Thanks! Are you okay with a manager position? It comes with a pay increase!"

"Yeah!"

"Cool. We'll start training when you come back from your vacation. So..." she said as she looked around the store, "since it's just the two of us today, we'll just do everything together. Go ahead and open a register. Keep an

eye on the customers. We'll alternate between the floor, the

dressing rooms, and restock as you see fit. Um..." she

tapped the countertop with her pen as she thought of what

to say next, "oh, yea... I'm going to let you go at six p.m.

Loyal is coming from six to ten. I'll stay and close with

him."

"Ok," I said with a smile.

Today was turning out to be a great day. I got CeCe

a job, I was getting a pay raise and a promotion and, to top

it off, I'd get to see Loyal. I had a big crush on Loyal. I

thought I was keeping how I felt about him to myself, but it

seemed like everyone I worked with knew except for

Loyal. There had been so many times I got caught staring at

him from across the room. I got so nervous when he came

around me; I started dropping things and tripping over my

own feet. It was so embarrassing and those darn butterflies!

I hated them.

"There you go again," Ami said, shaking her head and interrupting my thoughts.

"Huh?"

"You're doing it again," she said, as I cleared my throat.

"Doing what?" I replied as I picked up merchandise from behind the counter to place back on the sales floor.

"Daydreaming again with a big smile on your face. It's like every time someone says the name Loyal, your brain shuts down."

I tried to hide my embarrassment by putting clothes on hangers and checking the tags on the merchandise. "No. It doesn't."

"You can deny it all you want. The crazy thing is, he acts the same way you do. I still don't think he knows you like him," Ami laughed.

"What? You think he's feeling me?"

"What other reason is there for him to be checking your schedule every other week?"

"Nah ugh," I said, stunned.

Ami laughed. "Y'all are so young."

"We're not that much younger than you." I laughed.

"Hey. Give me those go-backs you're hanging up. I'll put them on the floor. Can you do me a favor? That mannequin in the window with the red cut out dress on. Can you take it off? We're sold out of that item. Here, put this two-piece on it," she handed me a different outfit. "A new shipment arrived, so let's get this advertised."

"Ok. No problem," I said as I hung up the last item and handed her a handful of go-backs. Just then, a customer approached the counter.

"Hi. Are you ready to check out?" I asked.

"Not, just yet. Can you tell me where I can find that red dress on the mannequin?"

"Oh. We're sold out. This is the last one."

"Could I have that one on the mannequin?"

"Sure. Let me check the size. What size do you need?" I asked as I checked the size on the mannequin.

"A small."

"You're in luck," I said as I undressed the mannequin. I handed her the dress.

"Thanks, I'll go try it on."

"Ok. If nobody is at the counter, just ring the bell when you're ready for us to ring you up."

"Will do. Thanks!" she said as she left the counter.

I grabbed the black split pants and the black cross crop halter top that Ami gave me and started dressing the mannequin. Just after I was done, I adjusted the mannequin properly in the window. I glanced out the window and did a double look. I could have sworn I saw Donnie drive by in a red car. It looked like a Dodge Charger. That was impossible. He was out with mama. I shook the feeling and continued working.

It turned out to be a busy shift and I lost track of time. As I fixed one of the clothes on the fixture, a familiar scent hit me and I closed my eyes. I felt someone poke me in my side and I jump, startled. I turned around to see Loyal. Time stopped; his cologne was so hypnotizing. His smile was mesmerizing. I wanted so badly to touch his smooth, honey-brown skin. I had the urge to find out just how smooth and soft his skin really was. His curly black hair was cut in a small fade. His brown eyes stared back at me.

"Ugh. You're doing it again," I heard Ami say as she walked past, getting me out of my daze and awakening the butterflies.

"Oh. Hey Loyal," I said as I knocked down three shirts from the rack and immediately bent down to pick them up. "It's six o'clock already?"

"Yeah. Just about. How has it been today?"

"Busy but good. We're short staffed, so it's just going to be you and Ami til closing."

"Yea, she kind of gave me a heads up after I clocked in," he said as he looked over at Ami, as she walked up to us and put her hand on my shoulder.

"Brie. Didn't you say you wanted to go to the state fair this year?"

"Yeah," I answered, looking at Ami

"You know it's open now, as of today."

"Um no, I—"

"That sounds like fun," Loyal cut me off and grabbed the clothes from me that fell. "I would love to take you if you don't mind."

I turned my gaze back to Loyal. *Did I hear him correctly?* I thought to myself.

"You're welcome!" Ami whispered in my ear as she turned to walk away, smiling. "Just don't call in and post any live videos. Y'all better go on your off day!" she yelled.

I watched her walk away and shook my head. She set me up.

"Well. I better get to work while Ami is in a good mood. How about I call you? We can set something up."

"Sure," I said as he gave me his phone, so I could type in my number. I quickly dialed my phone number and saved it to his contacts.

"Cool," he said, as I handed him back his phone.

"I just called you, make sure you save my number."

"Okay," I said, smiling.

"All right Brie. I guess I'll see you around."

"Yeah, see you later," I said as I walked to the back to clock out. I could not believe what just happened. *Ami think she was slick. I'm going to get her*, I thought to myself while smiling. Today turned out to be a great day!

I hurried home, excited to tell CeCe about her new job. I parked in front of the house and noticed a car parked across the street; it looked like Aunt Sherri's car. I hoped CeCe was with her if it was her car. I grabbed my keys and purse and got out of the car, making sure to lock the door. I rushed to the house, unlocked the door and turned the nob. As soon as I walked through, I felt a burst of energy run through my body. My arms and my legs were tingling. I took a deep breath, remembering the last time I had this feeling.

After catching my breath, I walked into the house and looked around; everything looked normal. I walked through the living room to the kitchen and saw Aunt Sherry sitting on a barstool laughing with a wine glass in her hand. Mama was standing across from her at the kitchen island with a wine glass in her hand. I walked in and put my keys on the key hook just above the counter.

"Hi Aunt Sherry. Hey Mama," I said as I turned to walk to my room. I sat my purse on my dresser and started undressing. I went, through my drawers for fresh panties, my black leggings, and my green sports bra. I ran across the hall to the bathroom for a quick shower. Luckily, the bathroom was right across from my bedroom. I put my braids up in a high bun before stepping in. The cool water felt so refreshing hitting my skin. It had been a hot and humid day, and the feeling of sweat and sticky skin had me feeling dirty all day.

My shower was fast. I was anxious to call CeCe and tell her about my day. I dried off before stepping out of the shower, making sure to dry my feet well before stepping on the bathroom rug. I hated wet floors; it was one of my biggest pet peeves. After drying off completely I hurried back to my room, lotioned up, and put my clothes on. *I'm missing something*, I thought to myself.

"Where's my deodorant?" I just had it sitting on my bed. I started searching for my deodorant, moving pillows, and checking on top of my dresser near my purse. "This is crazy. I just had it," I said to myself. I looked under the bed.

"There it is! How the heck did it get under the bed?"

As I reached for it, I spotted my cucumber melon body spray from Bath and Body Works. It was my favorite summertime fragrance. After spritzing myself, I put the deodorant on, put it in my top drawer, and tossed the body spray in my purse. I grabbed my phone and headed into the kitchen.

"Brenda! No! Tell me you didn't," Aunt Sherri said, laughing.

"I did!" My mom laughed. She was laughing so hard, she was crying.

"Wait, wait! That's not the worst part," she said as she waved her hand. "I get up to leave and there is tape stuck to my dress. I walk out with my right butt cheek showing; girl, I had on thongs!"

They were both laughing so hard, I couldn't help but to smile.

"What happened?" I asked, relieved to see my mom in a good mood after the way I left her this morning.

"I guess the joke was on me, huh?" my mom said, still laughing.

"Serves you right going off on her like that," Aunt Sherri said. She shook her head laughing, then took a sip of her wine. "Girl, this wine is good! I normally don't drink white wine. What is this called?"

"I know, right?" Mom said after she took a sip. "It's one of my favorites. It's called Castillo Del Poggio."

"This is nice!" Aunt Sherri said as she poured herself another glass of wine.

"It is. It's one of my favorites too," I replied.

"You let Brielle drink wine?"

"Not really but, then again, she is grown. She'll have a sip or two with me every blue moon, but she doesn't like alcohol. Supposedly, it gives her headaches."

"So, what's up with this Donnie guy? Did y'all just

come back from a date?"

"Um... I wouldn't call it a date. Brielle was supposed to hang out with us today, but she cancelled on me when she found out Donnie was going."

"Sorry," I said as I opened the fridge to pour myself a glass of cold mint tea. "I wanted a mother-daughter day."

"So, how do you feel about Donnie? Do you like him?" Aunt Sherri asked.

"Yea. I like him. I've only known him for a few weeks. We have been out on a couple of dates. I'm keeping my guards up though. He's too perfect."

"Perfect like how?"

"Always available, always happy, yet quiet. I guess you can say he has a mysterious side to him."

"Hey, Aunt Sherri, do you know if CeCe is coming over? I have some news I want to share with her?" I asked.

"Mysterious… in what ways?" Aunt Sherri asked as she took a sip of wine.

"He's never too far away."

"Well. He must stay near you," Aunt Sherry replied.

"Aunt Sherri!" I called out to her again. This time, I tapped her arm. She was cold.

"Your arm is cold! As hot as it is, why are you so cold?"

"Well, where does he stay?" asked Aunt Sherri.

"Mom, are you cold too?" I touched the side of her face. She was freezing. "Mom!" I shouted.

"He won't say. He only says he's from the area." My mom put her glass down. "You think that's a red flag?" my mom asked.

"Are you guys playing with me? Why are y'all

ignoring me? And why are both of you so cold when it's warm in the house?"

"Um…. yes! That's either your woman's intuition or your guardian angel. Whatever it is, you better listen to it."

"Hello!" I said in my mom's ear as I waved my hand up and down in her face. She didn't flinch.

"How does Brielle feel about him?" Aunt Sherri asked.

"I can't stand him. He gives me the creeps." I answered. I was still irritated that I was being ignored.

"I'm not sure. I haven't talk to her about him yet," my mom said.

"I just told you how I feel. Why are y'all talking as if I'm not here?" I asked, getting frustrated.

"Um… Brenda, we got to take this talk to the

family room. I'm missing my show," Aunt Sherri said after taking another sip of her wine.

"What show?" Mama asked.

"General Hospital. It's 1:25 p.m. I have already missed half of it," Aunt Sherri said while she pointed to the clock on the stove."

"It's not one- twenty f..."

I didn't even finish my sentence. The clock on the stove did say 1:25. *How is this possible? I got off of work at six o'clock this evening. It was six-seventeen when I pulled up*, I thought to myself out loud.

Just as my mom and Aunt Sherry left the kitchen, I saw CeCe's car pull up in front of the house. I ran to the door and threw it open. As soon as I stood outside the door, I felt as though someone hit me in the chest with a bag of bricks. I was in so much pain, I closed my eyes and dropped to my knees. I felt the tingling sensation move through my arms and legs. It reminded me of the feeling you got when your foot was asleep. My body felt so heavy.

I took a deep breath. When I opened my eyes, my hand was on the doorknob with my house key dangling from the door. I was standing in a position to walk into the house. I looked behind me, and CeCe's car was nowhere in sight. My purse was hanging from my shoulder, and I had on my work clothes.

"Talk about déjà vu!" I said to myself. I walked in the house and made my way through the living room and to the kitchen where Aunt Sherri was sitting on a bar stool with an empty wine glass next to her.

"Hi Brielle," my Aunt said.

"Hi Brie!" said my mom while she stirred ingredients in a pot.

"Hey Mama. Hi Aunt Sherri" I said as I placed my keys on the key hook above the countertop.

"Smells good!" I said as I kissed her cheek. Her skin was warm.

"Thanks, we are having red beans and rice tonight."

"Yummy," I said with a smile.

"You look sick baby. You okay?" my mom asked.

"Yeah. I just have a headache." I wasn't lying.

"Well,. go lay down and take some medicine. I'll let you know when the food is ready."

"Okay."

"You just missed Ciera; she left about fifteen minutes ago. She came over here looking for you. She didn't know you went to work today," my aunt said. "You can call her now. She bought her phone."

"Ok, I'll give her a call later," I said as I turned to walk to my room. I tossed my purse on the bed and sat down on the floor, leaning my back against my bed. I sat for a moment to try to formulate what just happened. I recalled the conversation my mom and Aunt Sherri were having.

After about ten minutes of thinking, I got up to take my clothes from my drawer so that I could go take a shower for the second time. After grabbing my black leggings and my green sports bra, I turn around to go take my shower and spotted my purse on the bed. Some items had spilled out from me tossing it. One of the items was my cucumber melon body spray hanging halfway out of my purse. Yep, I was in the past again but, this time, it was a more recent past.

5

Time seemed to slow down. After my shower, I just laid down on my bed and reminisced about my experience going back into the past. I think it was time for me to accept that this was happening for a reason. The first time this happened, I thought it was a coincidence, a one-time thing. Maybe even a dream until I read about Kitty and Frannie. That confirmed what happened to me really did happen. If only I knew why this was happening to me. *Am I supposed to learn something from the past or change something?*

I thought back to being lost in Mississippi. I was really scared and, at the same time, I was angry. I was angry about my decision to offer to go shopping. At the time, I felt like that was the worst decision I could have ever made. Being lost in Mississippi was life-threatening. I thought back to the conversation between Grandma Kitty and Grandma Frannie. Kitty must have been scared too.

Her decision to leave was not only a hard one but also life-threatening. It didn't seem like she regretted her decision. My thoughts were interrupted by the sound of my mom coming into the room.

"Brie... you awake?"

"Yeah."

"How are you feeling?"

"A little better," I said while sitting up in my bed. "My headache is not as bad. But it's still there. I guess I just got a lot on my mind."

"Like what?" she asked while she sat at the foot of the bed.

"You promise you won't get mad?"

"You're not pregnant. Are you?" Her voice sounded more stern.

"No, mama!"

"Okay." She exhaled, sounding relieved.

"So, what's going on? What are you stressing about?"

"Donnie, mom. I don't like him. I get a bad feeling every time he's around."

"How can you say you don't like somebody when you don't even know him?"

"I know mama, and I know you taught me never to judge people, and I don't. However, I can't ignore the fact that he throws off weird vibes. I don't want to get to know him."

"To be honest... I feel it too. There is something off about him." She shook her head while looking as if she was lost in her thoughts.

"Are you guys dating?" I asked, hoping she said no.

"No. He's just a friend. We went out a few times. He does have a baffling side to him. I don't know what it is. I can't quite put my finger on it."

"How did you two meet? Do you work together?"

"Yeah. Well, sort of. He's also a flight attendant. We just don't work for the same airlines. But, we do meet up a lot at our destinations."

"Is that normal? I mean, meeting up at the same destination with other flight attendants that work for other airlines as often as you meet up with Donnie?"

"No, that's one of the baffling things I was talking about. Yet, he aways is dressed in uniform and he seems very popular with the other flight attendants."

"Well. I still don't trust him. He grabbed me up this morning when I was leaving for work."

"What do you mean he grabbed you?" my mom

114

asked, raising her voice a bit.

"He grabbed my arm and squeezed it. He wanted to know where I was going."

"Why didn't you tell me sooner? What did you do?"

"I snatched my arm away, told him don't ever touch me again and that it was none of his business where I was going."

"Why didn't you tell me sooner?"

"I don't know mama; today has been a weird day for me," I said as I got out the bed and stretched.

"Well, maybe it's best if we do keep our distance from him. It doesn't sit right with me that he put his hands on my daughter. The food is ready. Are you hungry?" she asked, getting up from the bed.

"For your red beans and rice... yes!" I said, as we walked out of my room and down the hall followed by her.

My stomach was growling from the moment I came home from work. The aroma from the food she cooked traveled throughout the house. My hunger pain grew at the thought of finally getting to savor the meal she made.

"Where is Aunt Sherri?"

"She left about an hour ago. She pretty much been here all day." Mama already had our plates on the table. She made red beans and rice, greens, cornbread and chicken.

"Yum. This looks great! I missed your cooking," I said as I sat down at the table.

"I bet you did, cause Lord knows what you be trying to cook!"

"Mama!" I laughed "I can cook," I said as I took a bite of my chicken.

"If that's what you want to call it," she laughed.

"Watch. You'll see. I'm going to cook dinner for you next."

"I'm scared to ask," my mom said while laughing.

"I'm making gourmet hamburger helper."

"No!" She scrunched up her face. "There is nothing gourmet about hamburger helper."

I laughed, as she continued.

"Plus, I may have over did it. We have enough for leftovers. I forgot tomorrow is seafood Tuesday."

"Aww mom! I love seafood Tuesday," I said, disappointed.

"That's ok. We can do seafood for lunch," I said.

"That's a good idea. By the way, before I forget. I made dessert… your favorite!"

"No. Banana pudding!" I look around. "Where—"

"It's in the fridge," she cut me off before I could finish my sentence.

"You must have had a lot of time on your hands. I thought you went out with Donnie today."

"You mean after you left when I told you not to." She cut her eyes at me as she took in a fork of greens.

"Sorry," I said, looking down at my plate while I scooped up some red beans and rice. I did feel bad about leaving mama with Donnie. At the time, I just wanted to get back at her for changing our plans. Maybe I should have gave Donnie a chance. I was sure he felt the attitude I was giving him as soon as I opened the door. However, my mom and I did have a weird feeling about him. *That has to mean something*, I thought to myself.

"That's alright. I understand why you were upset. I was wrong. I got to remember you're not a kid anymore. I can't tell you not to go to work. Anyway, we went to the pancake house. When our food came, he said something came up. He paid for our food and left. He didn't even take his food with him, nor did he eat any."

"Who goes to a restaurant, orders and don't eat?" I asked while stuffing chicken in my mouth.

"My point exactly. That's that mysterious side of him or it could have been a legit emergency. But, what's crazy is he never took out his phone. So, I ended up eating by myself and left. I basically been home all day."

"That's so weird... you know, I could have sworn I saw him driving in the parking lot at Ami's today. What kind of car does he have?"

"A red... I think it's a Dodge," she said after taking a bite of her cornbread.

"Yep! I saw him driving a red Charger."

"No. It couldn't have been him. I didn't tell him

where you work. Maybe it's a coincidence."

"Maybe. Did he leave you stranded at the Pancake House?" I asked while getting up to get us a serving of banana pudding.

"No. I drove myself. Remember I told you I feel weird around him too. I'm not about to lock myself in his car."

I pulled out the bowl of banana pudding goodness. Perfect layers of pudding, bananas, Nilla, and custard. The smell and look of it made my stomach growl, as if I hadn't just eaten a full dinner. I spooned out a good size portion for the both of us. I made sure to put it back in the fridge before handing my mom her serving of dessert.

"So, when do you go back to work?" my mom asked as she dug into her desert.

"Wednesday. Ami gave me an extra day of vacation

since I went in today."

"Oh! That's nice of her. Well, why don't we have our girl's day out tomorrow. What do you say? Just the two of us like you planned."

"I don't know mama. I'm a very busy person. I'd have to check my calendar," I said as I picked up my cell phone from the table. She threw a crumbled-up napkin at me, and it hit me on my forehead.

'Brielle!" she laughed.

"I'm just playing mom. You have a good aim," I laughed while rubbing my forehead.

"Not really. I was aiming for your right eye."

"Yes, we can hang out tomorrow," I said, still laughing.

After dinner, we cleaned up the kitchen together. Mom went in the family room to watch a move, and I finally found the time to call CeCe. I walked back to my room while I dialed CeCe. Right before I pressed the call button, I got an incoming call from CeCe.

"Hey! I was just calling you."

"I know, I felt it and decided to beat you to it."

I shook my head. "How's everything going with your mom?" I asked as I laid back on my bed.

"The same! If she keeps messing with me, you're going to have another slumber party."

I could imagine CeCe was rolling her eyes at her last statement. That's all her and her mom did lately was argue. "Um. No! How you come to my house to get away from your mom and have me sleep on the floor while you sleep in my bed?"

"Well, you had fell asleep in the middle of the movie. It made no sense for both of us to sleep on the hard floor. I gave you a pillow and blanket."

"Well, the least you could have done was make up my bed before you left."

"I was going to make it up. I was going to do it later... I didn't want to wake you."

I shook my head while laughing. "CeCe! That's the dumbest excuse I ever heard. How would you wake me if I'm on the floor?" We both laughed. "Anyway, I got some good news for you."

"Really! I love good news, especially when it's for me. What's up?"

"How does it feel to be employed?"

"What?"

"I got you a job!"

"Brie. I thought you said you had good news. I

should have never called you. You play too much," CeCe said, sounding disappointed.

"I'm serious Ciera!"

"So, where do I supposedly work?"

"Ami's Boutique. With me."

"Stop playing. Are you for real?"

"Yep! Ami wants you to come in to submit an application tomorrow. She'll go over the job details with you and give you a tour."

"I don't need to do an interview?"

"Nope, I vouched for you. So, you better not make me look bad," I said, being serious.

"I'll go tomorrow morning. Thanks for looking out for me."

"Don't thank me, that's what family is for."

"So, if we're such good family, why did you lie to me?"

"What are you talking about? I never lied to you," I said, sitting up in my bed.

"I thought you was having a mother daughter day. I came over and found out you went to work."

"That was the plan. My mom invited Donnie at the last minute, so I got mad and went to work."

"Donnie! That guy we met at the airport?"

"Yes girl. I get a bad vibe around him. He grabbed my arm out of anger this morning while I was leaving for work."

"Wait, What?" CeCe said, raising her voice.

"Yep."

"First off, he doesn't know you enough to be

125

putting his hands his hands on you and, second, where was your mom? Does she know?" CeCe asked. I could tell she was starting to get angry.

"My mom was in her room getting dressed. Yeah, I told her just before dinner."

"What was he angry about?"

"Either at the fact I wasn't going out with him and my mom, or because she was calling for me and I was walking out."

"That still doesn't give him the right to touch you."

"Then, I could have sworn he drove by my job."

"Stalker!"

"Right!" I replied, laughing. "I told my mom I saw him. She thinks that could have been a coincidence. She never told him where I worked."

"You better keep your eyes and ears open. Let me know if I need to tell my dad," CeCe said.

"I will. But I don't see no reason to get Uncle Glen involved."

"If you say so. I'm about to go since I must report to work tomorrow. That doesn't even sound right coming from me." We both laughed.

"Okay. Well, talk to you later."

"Okay. Tell Apple I said hi!" CeCe said just before she hung up laughing. I looked at the phone and shook my head.

6

Brenda's POV:

"I can't believe Donnie put his hands on my

daughter," I thought to myself out loud while pouring myself a glass of red wine. I wanted something stronger, but I needed a clear head for when I talked to Donnie. The mysterious side to him had all types of alarms sounding. I felt like I needed to be very careful how I approached him. I didn't realize my hands were shaking until I took a sip of my wine. My heart was racing. I was livid.

"I could kill him!" I yelled out before downing the rest of my wine and pouring myself another glass. "Her own daddy had never put his hands on her. What makes Donnie think he has the right?" I said aloud as I walked to the living room and sat on Gerald's favorite chair. I put on his favorite movie, *Die Hard*. Usually, when I was upset or wanted to feel closer to Gerald, I sat in his chair and watched his movie. I felt my anger start to subside as I got more into the movie.

Halfway through the movie, my cell phone rang. I looked at the caller ID as I took another sip of my wine. It was Donnie. I stared at the phone as my anger returned with the sight of his name. I silenced the phone, knowing if I rejected the call, he would know. *I'll talk to him when I'm ready and not before*, I thought to myself as I put the phone down.

Once the movie was over, I turned the TV off, placed my wine glass in the sink and threw away the empty wine bottle. I walked to Brielle's room and cracked her door open to check on her. She hated when I did that. I'd been doing that since the day she came home from the hospital. I knew she was twenty-one now, but she was still and always would be my baby. Her safety was my number one concern. That's why I quit my job as a flight attendant. I'd been away for too long.

In two weeks, I'd start back as a marriage therapist. I couldn't wait to surprise Brielle. She thought I quit my career. I didn't; I just took a very long leave of absence for my mental health. After Gerald died, I no longer knew who

I was or what I was supposed to do with my life. I first met Gerald in the 4th grade. By 8th grade, he was my first real crush. By high school, we were high school sweethearts. We ended up getting married three months after graduating from college. Losing Gerald was the hardest thing I'd ever had to deal with. I'd known him my whole life. We grew up together.

The world started to look different to me. I had lost myself and I didn't want Brielle to see me that way. So, I became a flight attendant. I needed to get away from the house, the constant memory of him. I was starting to feel more grounded now, although the house was still decorated the same as it was since the last day Gerald was here, and all his clothes were still hanging in the closet and folded in his drawers. I thought I was ready to start making some changes.

I saw Brielle was sleeping, so I softly closed her door back and went to my room. I took a quick shower, flossed and brushed my teeth, put my blue pajama pants and white T-shirt on, stuffed my curls inside of my pink satin hair bonnet and sat down on the side of the bed. It was time for me to call Donnie now that I was calmer but, the moment I scrolled down to his name, I felt my heartbeat faster. My anger slowly started to come back. I tried to keep it at bay while I pressed call on my cell phone. It rang twice before he answered.

"I called you earlier. You didn't answer. I know you're at home. Why didn't you answer?"

I took my ear off the phone and looked at it as though the phone was growing arms and legs. This fool didn't even say hi when he answered. He just jumped straight into my business.

"Excuse me!" I said with attitude.

"I asked why didn't you answer? Where have you been? Did you leave the house? I just want to know where you been, that's all."

"Yeah. I heard you the first time. What I want to know is why you feel like you're entitled to know what I'm doing or where I'm going?"

"I just want to make sure you're safe. What's up with all this attitude in your voice?" he said as if he didn't understand why I would be upset by his questioning. I was getting more upset with every sound of his breath. I was ready to change the subject and end this conversation permanently.

"Listen, Brielle told me you grabbed her this morning when she was on her way to work."

"Yeah. She was about to fall. I grabbed her arm to try to catch her. She sounds ungrateful. Maybe I should've just let her fall."

"So. You are calling my daughter a liar?"

"Yeah! If she's telling you anything other than the truth. Maybe I need to come over and talk—"

"No. You are not welcomed anywhere near me, my daughter or my house," I cut him off.

"What are you saying? You need me!" His voice was getting louder yet, it was calm.

"Need you! We are not in a relationship," I laughed. "I don't even know you. Therefore, I don't need you," I continued.

"Brenda. I can see your upset. I'm going to let you calm down for a few days before I come through."

"Did you just hear what I said, Donnie? You come to my house, and I can guarantee you will not leave the same way you came."

"Is that a threat? Are you threatening me now?"

"I don't make threats."

"Oh. Ok. So, it's a promise," Donnie laughed and hung up the phone.

Yep. This fool was crazy. But, that's okay. He was about to meet my crazy. I didn't back down from anything or anyone, especially when it came to my daughter. I was going to have to inform Brielle to keep her guard up. I couldn't help this funny feeling that something as about to go down. I didn't know when or where. But, I was ready. I stayed ready!

7

I woke up to the deafening sound of crushing metal. I jumped out the bed and checked the house. All the windows were closed, yet the sound was so loud, I could have sworn the windows were open. I checked on my mom. She was still asleep. I walked around the house looking for something out of place. *Nope. Nothing out of place,* I thought to myself. The sound clearly came from outside. Maybe it was an accident.

Besides being woken up scared, I was excited to hit the town with mama. It had been way too long since we last had a mother-daughter day. We used to hang out together a lot more when my dad was around. I remembered how my dad used to turn on the music and let mama and I have a fashion show, our way of showing off the items we bought. I look over at the cupcake on my wall and smiled, wishing he was still here.

I was too excited to go back to sleep. I decided to shower and get dressed for the day. I decided to wear my purple ombre shorts with a purple sleeveless tank that read *Nope Not Today* in bold white letters and my white sneakers. I walked over to the mirror to fix my hair into a high bun and made sure to do a little something to my edges. I knew it was going to be hot today and I wanted to make sure all my hair was up.

Lastly, I made sure to spray on my cucumber melon body spay before heading to the kitchen to make us a light breakfast. I wanted to make sure we saved room for lunch since today was seafood Tuesday.

After cooking and making coffee, I fixed my mom's plate, placed all her food on a tray and made my way down the hall to my mom's room. I knocked on the door before walking in.

"Mommy. Time to get up," I said as I sat the tray

down in front of her king size bed on her dark-blue, velvet tufted bed bench. I was careful not to spill anything. My mom's bed sat between two white nightstands. A navy-blue lamp sat on top of both nightstands. There was a narrow wall-length window that both nightstands sat in front of. There was a large two panel wall-length window that was in the middle of the bedroom wall. Each window had white and navy-blue floor-length curtains attached to them. Navy-blue was my dad's favorite color. He and my mom were both partial to the same color. In one corner of the room was my dad's white six-drawer chest. My mom's seven-drawer dresser was in the middle of the room underneath the fifty-inch tv. The closet was in the step-down ensuite. I walked over to the window and opened the curtains, letting in the sunlight.

"No! Too bright," she said as she pulled the covers over her head.

"You're normally a morning person. What time did

you go to bed last night?"

"You mean this morning. I feel like I just closed my eyes. Ugh! I need my coffee," she said as she sat up in the bed.

"I got you covered!" I said as I went to grab the tray. "Here, I made you breakfast."

"Oh Lord! You cooked?"

"Mama, I can cook. Plus, anyone can make an egg and bacon sandwich," I laughed.

The first thing she reached for is the coffee and took a sip. I scrunched up my face. "That's disgusting! I still don't see how you drink your coffee like that."

"What? Black? I been drinking black coffee since you were little."

"I know. But that doesn't mean it's any less disgusting."

"Well. I don't drink it for the taste. It's healthy."

"Healthy or not, it's still disgusting."

Mama took another sip of coffee while looking at me. "I see you're dressed for the day. You look nice, but isn't it a bit early? What time is it?" she asked as she looked around for her phone. I glanced at the clock on the dresser.

"It's thirty minutes till ten. Most places open at ten. So, no, I'm not dressed early. You're just late," I laughed as I turned to leave the room. "I'm going to go eat."

"Okay," she said as she sipped more coffee while reaching for the remote control to her tv.

As I walked back to the kitchen to fix my plate, I shivered. I could feel goosebumps on my arms. I got the feeling I was being watched. I shook the thought away. So much had happened since Mississippi. I felt I was always paranoid now, wondering if and when was the next time I was going to feel that burst of energy again. I sat at the bar with my plate and decided to text CeCe.

Me: Good morning. Are you up yet?

I took a bite of my sandwich and waited for her to reply. It didn't take long before my phone alerted me of a message.

CeCe: Yeah, I'm up. Good morning. I'm getting ready to go to Ami's. What time do they open?

Me: She opens at 10 a.m.

CeCe: Okay. I'm just about ready

Me: What are you wearing?

CeCe: Black pants, white shirt

Me: Are you nervous?

CeCe: Yea... very. This is my first job. What if I

say something wrong?

Me: Well. Remember it's not an interview. You already have the job. She's just going over your duties, pay and giving you a tour of the store

CeCe: Ok. Well, if I leave now, I'll get there just before she opens. So. I'll let you know how it goes. TTYL

Me: Okay

After I finished my breakfast sandwich, I grabbed my plate and walked to my mom's room. I knocked on the door but no answer. I walked into an empty room. I heard the shower running from her ensuite. I grabbed her tray and headed back to the kitchen to wash out our plates. As I walked down the hallway, I felt goosebumps on my arms again. I shivered as I reached the sink and cut the water on.

"Pay attention."

"Huh? Mama... did you say something?"

There was no answer. I cut the water off and looked around. It seemed like somebody was right next to me. I turned around and leaned back against the counter while looking around. I knew I was being paranoid, but I just couldn't shake the feeling that I was being watched.

8

Ciera's POV

I wish I could say I wasn't nervous, but I was. I loved shopping at Ami's Boutique. I was okay with using Brielle's discount whenever I had money to do some shopping. Now that I worked there with my own employee discount, my paychecks were already gone. I just hoped everything Brielle said was true. I stood in front of my mirrored closet door to check myself one last time before I left. My hair was brushed into a neat high bun, edges laid as always. I had on a white V-neck blouse, black high-waisted pants and my black flats.

I smiled at the reflection I saw in the mirror. I grabbed my phone to take a quick selfie. Afterwards, I grabbed my keys and purse. I cracked open my door and peeked up and down the hallway. My parents were nowhere to be seen, so I quickly ran down the stairs into the living room and peeked around the corner into the kitchen.

"All clear!" I whispered to myself before making a dash to the front door. Once I was outside the front door, I yelled, "Mom, Dad, I'm leaving. Bye!" then quickly closed the door and ran to my light-blue Honda Civic. I didn't want my parents to know where I was going. I didn't want them to know I had a job until I knew I had a job. No need to get their hopes up.

The ride to Ami's Boutique was quicker than I wanted. I was so nervous, I was actually enjoying the ride. I arrived five minutes to ten. Brie said they unlocked the doors at ten. So, I sat in the car listening to music while I looked at the different stores. This was a small shopping center. Ami's was the only clothing store in the shopping center. There was also a phone store, party supply, donut shop, vitamin store and a small bistro that served the best chicken quesadillas I'd ever had in my life. Between Ami's and this little bistro, I was destined to remain broke.

I looked back at Ami's just as someone unlocked the door. I looked quickly at the clock on my dashboard. "That was the quickest five minutes of my life," I thought out loud.

Though I'd hated to admit it, I was glad time was moving fast. I hated my stomach being in knots. I wanted to hurry up and get this over with. I quickly cut the car off, grabbed my purse and got out the car. I looked at my reflection through my car window, making sure nothing was out of place.

Once inside, I walked over to the sales counter. After noticing there was nobody behind the counter, I turned around to browse the store for a worker. The store was neat and clean, every clothing fixture alike lined up in a perfect row. Every mannequin placed perfectly in the windows and randomly around the store dressed to impress with wigs on. Being the type of person I was, I was automatically drawn to the circular clothing rack right in front of me. I was so fascinated with the two shirts that I found that I didn't notice that there was now someone behind the counter.

"Finding everything ok?"

"Oh... um, I'm not even supposed to be shopping. I'm actually looking for Ami," I said as I put the two shirts back on the rack.

"She's in her office, follow me. What's your name?" she asked as she led me to the back of the store.

"Ciera"

"Nice to meet you, Ciera. I'm Jessica." She smiled.

"Do you have an interview?"

"To be honest, I'm not sure."

146

She gave me a confused look and continued to lead me down a hallway to a door at the end of the hall. She knocked three times and cracked the door open.

"Hey Ami. There's a Ciera here to see you."

"Great. You can let her in. Thanks Jessi!"

"No problem. Good luck!" Jessica said to me before turning and leaving. I walked into the office.

"Hello Ciera. Nice to finally meet you," Ami said while holding out her hand for me to shake. Ami wore her purple and black locs in a barrel roll updo. She had on white pants with a black long-sleeve sheer shirt and a thin purple tank underneath.

"Wow. I love your hair!" I said as I shook her hand.

"Thank you! Go ahead and have a seat," she said as she pointed to the two chairs in front of her desk. "Thank you for coming by to see me so quickly!"

"Well, thanks for having me," I said.

"So. Tell me a little about yourself. Are you in school?"

"Yes."

"What are you majoring in?"

"I'm unsure. I'm still undecided at the moment."

"Well. That's ok. You have time. Do you have any retail or customer service experience?"

I could feel my heartbeat racing. Brie lied! This was an interview. Ugh! I never had an interview before. I was not ready. *I hope she don't ask me for a resume,* I thought to myself before answering. "Um... no. I don't. This would be my first job."

"Okay. That's exciting!" She smiled as she leaned

back against her chair. "Brielle told me this is one of the places you like to shop at. It's weird that I've never met you before."

"I know. I definitely would have remembered you."

"So. What's your availability?"

"On the weekdays, I'm free in the evenings and, on weekends, I'm free all day."

"Okay. I can work with that," Ami said while nodding her head. "Well. The starting pay is seventeen twenty-five an hour. You will also be receiving vacation and sick pay. We also offer healthcare if you decide you want it. You would be filling our sales associate position. Your job would be to ring up the customers, clean and monitor the fitting rooms, and restrooms. Make sure the sales floor is clean, pick up any clothing that was tossed on the fixtures or have fallen onto the floor. Restock the merchandise and so on. Do you think you can handle that?"

"Will I have to do all of that by myself?"

"No. You will have other associates on the floor with you during our shifts. Your duties will be divided. However, at some point, you will have experience doing everything within the job description."

"Oh! Okay. Sorry."

"No problem. I understand this is your first job. Do you have any questions regarding the position?"

"Yes. Do you have a dress code?"

"Good question! Black pants, white or black tops. The outfit you have on today is a perfect example. Business casual."

I smiled and nodded my head. "Is it a set schedule?" I asked.

"No. The schedules come out every two weeks. So, your off days will switch around. But, for the most part, I try to stay within your availability. If there's ever any issues or changes in your availability, just let me know or the manager on duty."

"Will do," I said.

"Great! So, how do you feel about becoming part of our team here at Ami's?"

"Awesome! I would love to. Thanks!" I said with a smile.

"Perfect. Let me give you a tour of our store. Then, we'll come back, and I'll have you fill out some paperwork," Ami said as she stood up and got ready to lead us out the office.

"Sounds good," I said as I stood up to follow her. We made a right coming out the office. It was a short hallway with three doors.

"This door to the left is our storage room," she said

as she opened the door. The room was surprisingly big. Things were scattered across the room, but I could tell it was organized.

"Here is where we keep extra fixtures for the clothes, our z-racks, our wall display equipment, hangers and additional mannequins," she said as she pointed to the left side of the room. She pointed to the middle of the room.

"This is where we keep our new merchandise that have not hit the floor yet, and over here are the items that are on the floor. When you need to restock or grab a different size for a customer, it would be here," she said, pointing to the right side of the room. There was also a brown desk in the front corner of the room with a telephone on the desk. Next to that was also a copier and fax machine.

"It may seem a bit much, but you will become very familiar with this room," she said as she cut the light off and we exited the storage room. "That door over to the left at the end of the hall leads to the back parking lot. Sometimes, when we get deliveries, they come through this door. There is a doorbell that you can also hear from the front of the store. Otherwise, they may drop of deliveries in the front." Ami's pointed to the door directly in front of us.

"This door here is an extra bathroom. There is a shower in there if you ever need to use it. The main bathroom that everyone uses is across from the fitting rooms, I'm sure your aware of that one."

"Yes, I am."

We walked back down the hallway towards her office but made a left at the corner. Different picture frames lined the walls of the hallway. We entered a big open room.

"This is our breakroom."

To the left of the room was counter space with a

sink. There were two microwaves placed on the counters and a fridge. There were two vending machines near the fridge: one with food and snacks, the other with drinks. There was a flat screen tv mounted to the wall and a black sofa in the center of the room. Behind the sofa and off to the side was a nine-seater dining room table. On the right end of the room, the wall was lined up with lockers.

"You're welcomed to any unused locker. Just make sure to bring your own combination lock. Here is where we post the schedules and any upcoming news or events." She pointed to a bulletin board on the wall just next to the door.

"This is where you clock in and out. It scans your face to clock you in and out. We'll get you set up for this system tomorrow." She pointed to a small system on the wall. "Let's head back to my office, and I'll get you started on your paperwork. Usually, you fill out an application before you're hired," she laughed.

When we got back to the office, I took a seat in one of the chairs. Ami went to a file cabinet in the corner of the room and pulled out several sheets of papers. She walked back to her desk and handed them to me.

"Here you go. This one is the application. I still need to have this on file for you, and these are for taxes. Let me know if you need any help. By any chance, do you have your social security card with you?"

"Yes, I have it."

"Perfect. Can I borrow your card and your photo ID to make a copy?"

"Sure," I said as I gave her the documents. It took me about thirty minutes to finish with all the paperwork. The tax forms were so confusing; it was like trying to understand a foreign language. After handing Ami the paperwork and double checking to make sure I put away my ID and card, I stood up to leave and so did Ami. She

155

held out her had for me to shake.

"Welcome to the team! Are you alright with starting tomorrow at 4 p.m.?"

"Yes. That's fine," I said while shaking Ami's hand.

"Great! Your training starts tomorrow. Do you remember the way out?" Ami asked before sitting back down.

"Yes, I do."

"Okay! Well, you have a great rest of the day and I'll see you tomorrow."

"You too! Bye," I said as I turned to leave. I walked out her office with a big smile on my face. I couldn't believe I had a job. Wait till my parents found out! I couldn't wait to get home, so I could tell them the good news.

As soon as I turned the corner coming onto the sales floor, I spotted Donnie. He had on dark blue jeans and a white t-shirt. He looked upset, unraveled, as if he didn't get any sleep. When I first met Donnie, he looked good, kept together. Looking at him now, his clothes were wrinkled and his hair looked as if he had been pulling it out. There was pieces of his locs missing. You could clearly tell he hadn't washed his face. He had crust near his eyes and a dry slob mark near the corner of his mouth. He was visibly upset. He was walking through the store mumbling to himself. I remembered the talk I had with Brie the night before. I quickly ducked behind the clothing fixtures, watching him from the side. Luckily, it didn't look like he saw me.

What should I do? I thought to myself. I could go back to Ami's office, but this man could be crazy enough to go back there. I could go out the back door, but I would have to walk far to get to my car. Plus, he could spot me if he left while I was walking to my car. I dodged around the fixtures as he came my direction and slowly made my way to the front exit. *God, I hope none of my coworkers saw me. They'll think I'm crazy before they even get a chance to know me*, I thought to myself.

Donnie was still walking towards the back of the store. He peeked down the hall towards Ami's office, then disappeared into the hallway. It was a good thing I decided not to go back to her office. I took the opportunity to make a run for it. I dashed out the store and to my car. I hit the unlock button on the key fob as I approached the car. I started it up and reversed. I spotted Donnie in the store window just as I put the car in drive and pulled off.

I could understand those vibes Brie was talking about. I definitely needed to talk to Brie but not before I told my dad. This man had clearly lost his mind. God knows what he would have done if Brielle was at work.

9

Today was amazing! I thought to myself as I closed my eyes and leaned back in my chair while I enjoyed my massage and the warm bubbly water as I soaked my feet. We shopped, played miniature golf and had lunch at Ray's Seafood Kitchen. I was surprised when mama drove us to a shooting range. She taught me how to load and unload a gun and how to shoot. I never knew my mom knew how to handle a gun. Her aim was on point. She said my dad taught her. He had planned on teaching me after I turned eighteen.

Right now, we were relaxing while getting a manicure and pedicure.

"Why are you over there smiling?" my mom asked.

"Just thinking about today. I'm having so much fun, I don't want it to end."

"Well, too bad you have to go to work tomorrow. Otherwise, we wouldn't have to end our evening early," she said as she lifted her foot for the nail technician.

"We don't have to end it this early. Let's do something else after this. What about bowling?"

"You want to go bowling after getting our nails done?"

"Oh right," I said, kind of disappointed.

"Let's do a movie!" Mom said.

"Okay. What do you want to see?" I asked, trying not to laugh as the technician scraped the bottom of my foot.

"Let's be spontaneous. We'll see what's playing and the times when we get there." I looked at my mom and turned my head to the side, smiling.

"Mom! I haven't seen this side of you in a long time. Normally, you have to have everything planned out."

Mom smiled. "Yeah, I know. It feels good!"

"What changed?"

"I don't know. I think I finally realized I can live a life without your father. It took me almost three years to accept the fact he's no longer here." I looked at my mom while she spoke.

"Do you blame me, mama?" I asked while looking down at my feet while the technician prepped to polish my toenails. I was looking for any excuse to not show my mom the tears that were about to fall from my eyes.

"Blame you for what?"

"For daddy dying."

"Why would I blame you? It wasn't your fault. Do you blame yourself?" she asked with concern in her voice.

"Well, Mom, how can I not? I keep telling myself that if only I would have taken the time to search for that stupid box of tampons, he would still be here today."

"No, sweetheart. Stop that! It wasn't your fault. It was just his time."

I shook my head no and looked at my mom, letting her see the guilt running down my cheeks. "I feel like when the family looks at me, they see me as the killer. It started with you, Mama! You couldn't even stay in the same house as me after I found that box of tampons in the closet. You become a flight attendant of all things," I cried. My mom grabbed my hand.

"No, baby, that wasn't it at all!" I could see my mom's eyes watering up. "Brie, I didn't leave because of you. I left because of your dad. I have known Gerald basically my whole life. I grew up with him, seen him every day at school starting in 4th grade. By the 8th grade, he was my first real crush. By high school, we were high school sweethearts. We ended up getting married three months after graduating from college. We started our life together very young. Always made decisions together. Once your dad died, I felt like I was losing control of my life. I didn't know how to live in a world without him in it. I was trying to be strong for you but, at the same time, I was losing my mind. I didn't want you to see me like that. Every piece of furniture in that house reminded me of your dad. I didn't have the strength to redecorate or even box up his clothing. It was driving me insane being in that house. So, I found a job that would take me away from the house so I could heal. Now, I see that was the wrong decision. I left you while you were still grieving too. I'm sorry that I wasn't there for you, Brie," she said as she kissed my hand.

In a way, I felt relieved. All this time, I thought it was the sight of me that made my mom leave. I wasn't mad at her. How could I be? For the past three years, we both had been fighting our own issues surrounding the death of my father, her husband, her soulmate. I guess there was no wrong way to grieve a loss.

"I'm here now," she continued.

"Only for two weeks," I stated.

"Well, not necessarily. I was going to surprise you. But you need to know now. I quit my job as a flight attendant. I'm going back to work as a marriage therapist. So, no, I'm not going anywhere," she said as she squeezed my had. Before I could respond to her, my phone rang.

"It's CeCe."

"Go ahead and answer." She let go of my hand.

"Hello."

"Hey Brie!" CeCe answered.

"So, how did it go?" I asked.

"It went great. I start tomorrow at four p.m. Do you work tomorrow?"

"That's good! See, I told you. Yeah, I work from ten till four p.m. tomorrow."

"Aw. I was hoping we'd work together."

"We will. Ami's training me for the manager position starting tomorrow."

"Manager! So, you're about to be my boss?"

"Yep," I said, popping the P sound.

"I'm telling you now. If you fire me, I'm telling your mom. Plus, my mom will kill you!" she laughed.

"Right! I do not want to get on your mom's bad side. Did you tell your parents yet?" I asked, laughing.

"Yeah. Girl, my mom ordered pizza! She been all smiles since I told her. Now, she trying to plan a mother-daughter day."

I laughed and glanced over at my mom. She was on the phone too. I could tell it was a serious conversation by the hard expression on her face.

"Don't be surprised if my mom shows up at your house with gifts and a cake," CeCe continued. "She couldn't stop talking about how grateful she is to have you around."

"How did your dad take it?"

"He was shocked, then happy. But, now, he's worried."

"Worried about what?" I asked while giving the nail technician my other hand. Luckily, I had my Bluetooth headset in my ear.

"Listen. I know you told me not to tell my dad about Donnie, but I did."

"What! Why? I don't need Uncle Glen worrying about nothing!" I said, annoyed.

"It's not nothing! He put his hands on you, and he came to Ami's today looking for you."

"What?" I asked, sitting up in my chair.

"Yeah. You heard me right. He was visibly upset, mumbling to himself. Girl, he looked a mess. He even went to the back towards Ami's office."

"Are you serious?"

"It's no telling what that man would have done if you were there. I had to hide behind the fixtures and sneak out before he saw me." I just sat with my mouth open, taking in everything CeCe was telling me. "What did you do to him?" she asked.

168

"CeCe, let me call you back." I hung up before she could reply. I looked at mama. She was still on the phone. Our nails were finished. We were sitting while they dried.

"Mama!" I called out to her. She looked at me and put up her index finger, signaling to wait a moment.

"Okay. Thanks. I'll let her know," she said before hanging up the phone.

"Mama! Ciera said Donnie came to my job today looking for me. She said he was upset."

"I know. That was Glen on the phone," she replied.

"Why was he looking for me? Why is he upset with me? I didn't do anything to him."

"Calm down Brie. I should have told you this sooner. I spoke to Donnie last night. I kind of went in on him for grabbing you up. He said you was lying. He says

169

you were about to fall, and he was trying to stop you from falling—"

"I wasn't falling!" I said, cutting her off.

"I know. I believe you. Anyway, I told him not to come around us or our home. He didn't take it too well."

"So, now he's blaming me for breaking y'all up? What is he going to do to me?" I asked worriedly.

"He's not going to do anything, and we were not a couple. There was nothing to breakup. Everything is going to be okay. Try not to worry too much," she said in a calming voice.

"Mama. It wasn't a coincidence that he drove by my job. He's stalking me. How else do you explain him coming to my job? Oh, my God! Will I have to quit? I just got promoted. I'm not safe at…"

"Brielle! Calm down!" my mom yelled, snapping me out of my panic mode. "I would never let anything happen to you. Plus... Glen already spoke to Ami. Starting tomorrow, Ami is going to be having security present during operating hours," she said as she started gathering her purse and slid her feet into her thong sandals we bought at the nail shop. I followed her lead and got ready to leave. I fished around my purse before pulling out my wallet.

"Mama, I'll pay for our nails since this was my idea."

"Are you sure?"

"Yeah. It's my treat," I said before walking over to the counter to take care of the bill. Mama followed close behind me.

"Do you still want to catch a movie?" she asked.

"Yea! Anything to get Donnie off my head. I refuse to let him ruin our time together again," I replied.

"Well. Since the movies was my idea, I'll pay for our tickets," she said.

After paying for our services, we walked to my mom's white Lincoln Navigator. My mom had been driving SUV's since I could remember. I never could understand way she needed so much space when we were only a family of three. She always said she felt cramped in cars, and she didn't like the feeling of being low to the ground. My mom wouldn't even step foot in my Nissan Maxima, and it was not even a small car. Well, to me it's not. We both walked to her truck in silence, both of us probably having Donnie on our minds. I felt a little better knowing that Ami would start having security at her store.

"So, do you want to grab a bite before we go to..."

"I would love to!" Donnie said, coming from around the back of my mom's truck and interrupting her sentence.

We stopped in our tracks. My heart started to race. This man looked horrible. His clothes were winkled, his shirt was half tucked, his pockets were empty and turned out, and we could smell liquor on his breath.

"What are you doing here, Donnie?" my mom asked with anger in her voice.

"I was in the neighborhood," he said while leaning against the back of my mom's truck, smiling. "I didn't expect to see you two. Mind if I tag along?" he continued with a smile on his face.

"Yes. We do mind!" I spoke. Donnie cut his eyes at me.

"I wasn't talking to you."

"But I'm talking to you," I replied as my mom pulled me back, looking at me with a smile on her face.

"Brenda, you didn't teach your daughter to respect her elders?"

"Oh, I taught her everything she needs to know."

"Well, you certainly didn't teach her not to lie," Donnie said, looking at me up and down as if I disgusted him.

"Well, somebody should have taught you how to recognize when your presence is unwanted! Don't you have anything else better to do than to bother us?" I said with anger in my voice while taking a step towards him.

"Brielle!" my mom yelled at me while pulling me back. "Let me handle this."

"Learn your place little girl!" Donnie said.

174

"How about I show you where your place is?" I said while taking a step to him, only for my mom to push me back. I was so angry, I was seeing red. I was raging. I was pacing back and forth, ready to pounce on him at any moment. I knew he was naturally stronger than me, but I was up for the challenge. I may not be able to fully take him, but I could for damn sure do some damage. I was ready to let him know I was not to be taken lightly.

Donnie looked at me with that same stupid smile that seemed to never leave his face. "She's feisty! I like that."

"Stay away from us, Donnie!" my mom warned. "Brie. Get in the truck," my mom ordered.

I walked slowly around Donnie, wishing he would do something to give me a reason to strike. Just as my mom started walking towards the driver side door, Donnie took a step and reached out, trying to grab my mom's right arm.

My mom quickly blocked his reach with her left hand. I quickly grabbed the arm she blocked, hyper-extending it while she took her elbow to his throat. Together, we shoved him onto the back of the truck with so much force that not only did the truck sway forward, I just knew there was going to be a dent that would forever remind us of this situation.

"I told you to stay away from us!" Mom yelled.

Donnie tried to laugh while looking back and forth between my mother and me with red eyes. "Wow! Like mother like daughter. Is this supposed to scare me?" he asked with a distorted voice.

"It should," my mother replied calmly.

"No. But I am intrigued." He gave her that futile smile that seemed to be plastered to his face.

"Stay away from us!" my mom said as she pressed her elbow into his neck more before releasing. I followed her release. Donnie's hand immediately went to his throat as he rubbed out the pain.

"We need to talk," he said.

"There's no we, Donnie. Never was. Brie, get in the truck."

I walked around to the passenger side door. By the time I got inside, my mom was inside as well. Donnie was yelling, "We need to talk," as we closed and locked the doors. I could tell he didn't like to be ignored. He started hitting the windows with his fist.

"Dammit! Open the door. We need to talk!" he yelled and kicked the side of the truck, as my mom started it up.

"We need to talk Brenda, open the door! Now!" He ran to my side of the window from the front of the truck as we start backing up. He banged on the window.

"This is your fault, Brielle! You ruined everything. Just tell the truth! You can fix this!" he yelled as he hit my window one last time before smiling. As we pull off, he yelled out, "This isn't over!"

"Are you okay?" my mom asked, as we made a right out of the shopping center.

"Yeah," I said as I looked at the side mirror. Donnie was standing in the middle of the parking lot watching us as we turn onto the street. "Ugh! What is wrong with that guy?" I asked, annoyed at the sight of him.

"It worries me how he found us. Glen said CeCe saw him at Ami's when she was leaving. She left a little after twelve p.m. Do you remember what time we left the house?"

"Around eleven-ish. You think he put a tracker on us?" I answered.

"Yeah. But if he did, why would he show up at Ami's knowing you wouldn't be there? We're in Scottsdale, at a random nail salon. There's no way he was just in the area." I could tell my mom was trying to piece things together.

"You think Uncle Glen could help?"

"Oh definitely! No doubt about it. I'll call him tomorrow, have him do a sweep for any cameras or listening devices that may be hidden in the house."

"And our cars," I added. "This is crazy! I feel like we're in a Lifetime movie or something," I said, leaning back in my seat in disbelief at what just happened.

"Are you still up for a movie?" my mom asked.

"We shouldn't let that 'thing' ruin the rest of our evening."

"Okay, you still want to grab a bite to eat?" Mom asked.

"To be honest, I'm not that hungry right now, but I know I'll be later. You want to sneak it in?" I asked with a smile.

"Brielle! You know you can't bring food into a movie theater. You think my purse is big enough?"

I laughed. "Yeah."

"Empty it out," she said, as we pulled into a burger joint.

We ordered two burgers and nuggets to share. We decided to get our drinks from the concession stand. On the way to the movies, I got a text message. I was surprised to see it was from Loyal.

Loyal: Hey! You busy?

Me: Not yet I'm on my way to see a movie with my mom

Loyal: I missed you at work today

Me: Really!

"Ugh!" I palmed myself on the forehead. Why would I send that?" I said out loud.

"What's wrong with you?" my mom asked.

"This guy that I been crushing on for months finally text me. He said he missed me at work today."

"So. What's wrong? Is that a problem?"

"No. It's my response that's the problem."

"What did you say?"

"I responded back *Really!* Ugh, I sound so desperate."

"You said you have been crushing on him for months?"

"Yeah."

My mom laughed, "Then, you are desperate."

"Mom!" I laughed as I received another text message

Loyal: Lol, yeah time moves slower when you're not there trying to hide from me

Me: I don't be trying to hide. I just be busy

Loyal: Yeah. Ok! Lol. You want to go out tomorrow?

Me: Sure, what do you have in mind?

Loyal: Bowling, the fair, out to eat, it's up to you. How about you decide on a place and let me know tomorrow when I pick you up?

I couldn't help but to smile.

Me: Ok, I work tomorrow though. I get off at four pm

Loyal: Cool. Send me your address and I'll see you tomorrow at six pm

I sent Loyal my address with a big smile on my face. I couldn't believe I was going out with Loyal tomorrow.

"Um... you're smiling so hard, my cheeks hurt," my mom laughed.

"I have a date tomorrow!"

"What's his name?"

"Loyal."

"I really hope he lives up to his name."

"Mom. Please don't tell him that when you see him tomorrow. I'm sure he hears that a lot," I begged. Mama laughed.

"I'll go easy on him."

We finally pulled into the parking lot for the movie theater and made sure we parked in a lit area in case Donnie decided to make another appearance.

"Are you sure they don't check bags when you go in?"

"Some theaters do. But this one doesn't"

We ended up picking a movie that started within two minutes. I was glad we made it but, after getting our drinks and popcorn at the concession stand, we missed almost ten minutes of previews. I hated missing previews.

The movie lasted two hours and fifteen minutes. Afterwards, we headed home. The day was finally catching up to me. It was just after nine o'clock and I was beyond tired. I hated that our day was ending but I was excited about my date tomorrow. I started dozing off on the ride home; the sound of my mom's beautiful singing voice was not helping me to stay awake.

I woke up when I noticed the truck had stopped moving, and her singing had stopped. I opened my eyes and looked at my mom. She was frowning while staring at something. I noticed that we were stopped in the middle of the street. I was so tired, I felt a little disoriented, not recognizing where we were. I followed her gaze to the front of our house. I sucked in a breath, not believing what I was seeing.

10

Our door was wide open, and the front room window was broken. Mama pulled into the driveway and cut the car off.

"Brie. Call Glen. Tell him to get here quick. I'm calling the cops," she said as she pulled out her phone, and I did the same. My mom had the phone to her ear as she got out the car.

"Mom! You're not going in. Are you?"

She didn't answer me. I could hear she was on the phone with a nine-one-one operator. I quickly scrolled down to Uncle Glen's phone number and pressed call while keeping an eye on my mom. If she decided to go in the house, I was going with her. After about four rings, Uncle Glen picked up.

"Hey Brie. What's going on?"

"Uncle Glen. Somebody broke into our house," I said, trying not to panic. I was wide awake now.

"Shit! I'm on my way. Yawl didn't go inside, did you?"

"No. But mama is standing in front of the house. She hasn't gone inside yet."

"Tell her not to. I'll be there in two minutes. Tell her to call the police," Uncle Glen said before hanging up the phone.

I got out the truck just as my mom hung up the phone. "Uncle Glen said he'll be here in two minutes."

"The police will be here in ten," she replied, sounding like she was in a trance. She took a step towards the house. I quickly stepped in front of her.

"Mama. Uncle Glen said not to go into the house."

She slowly turned her gaze to me. For a moment, I could see hurt. Then, it quickly switched to anger.

"This is my house!" she yelled out, not at me but more so in frustration.

"I know, Mama. But can we just wait for Uncle Glen... please?" She turned her gaze back to the house. "Just two minutes Mama. Come on. Let's wait in the truck," I said as I pulled her towards the truck. I opened the passenger side front door, and she reluctantly slid into the seat. I quickly closed the door and slid into the back seat. Both of us stared at the house in silence.

"Do you think he—"

"I'm going to kill him," she said, cutting me off.

"We have to be sure it was him, Mama."

She looked at me with tears in her eyes. At this point, I was not sure if they were tears of anger or hurt, maybe a little of both.

"We've been in this neighborhood for years Brielle, and nothing like this has ever happened before. All of a sudden, Donnie comes into the picture, starts acting a fool and then this happens. Do you remember what he said when we were leaving the shopping center? He said, this isn't over. This is his doing."

Uncle Glen arrived at the two-minute mark, just as he said he would. He pulled his black GNC Yukon on the side of the street in front of the house. He and a passenger got out of the truck. I recognized the passenger as Mike, Uncle Glen's right-hand man. Mike was tall, scary-looking but handsome. His skin was a rich dark brown color; he was clean cut and very muscular. He stood to be about six feet five inches tall. His physique and demeanor demanded respect. He was very quiet, always observant.

Tonight, he was dressed in a black suit and tie. Uncle Glen was not far off. He was muscular as well. He was a little shorter than Mike, standing at six feet four inches tall. His curly hair cut into a short fade; his goatee always trimmed thin. He had the same cinnamon-colored skin tone and green eyes like CeCe. He wore a dark gray suit pants and vest, with a black shirt and black trilby hat. They were both dressed to impress.

Once they got out the car, we started getting out of the truck. Mike started walking towards the house with his gun drawn. Uncle Glen held up his hand to us and told us to wait right there as he hurriedly walked up to catch up to Mike. He and Mike entered the house together, both with their guns drawn. After a few minutes of us waiting, the lights in the house came on. Uncle Glen yelled for us to come from the doorway.

When mama and I entered the house, our mouths dropped open. Mama screamed out in anger. All our furniture was tossed. The TV was smashed, all our dinnerware was tossed out of every cabinet, the cabinet doors left open, and dinnerware broken was all over the kitchen and dining room. I also noticed pieces of shattered glass in the living room, which was from the window being busted. You could hear pieces of glass shattering more with every step you took. All the pictures that were hanging on the wall in the hallway were thrown and shattered. One family portrait had my dad torn out of it. Looking at the torn photo proved to me that this was Donnie's doing.

When we entered my mom's room, the sight before me brought tears to my eyes. Her dressers were turned over, mirrors shattered. The comforter on her bed was removed, and there was a big yellow spot in the center of the mattress that held a strong smell of urine. My dad's dresser was lying off to the side with all his drawers removed and his clothes thrown out and cut up. The bed bench was thrown across the room. It was sliced across the top and cotton was coming out. The room was cold from the night air. The double window was broken, and the curtains were blowing in the wind.

We walked into the ensuite. My mom's bathtub was overflowing. Water flooded the floor. Luckily, she had a step-down ensuite, so the water didn't reach the bedroom carpet. There was writing on the mirror in black marker. There were words, but we couldn't make out what they meant. Words with backwards letters and symbols.

I ran to my room. The only thing to me that mattered was my cupcake wall decal. That's the only thing I had that I felt couldn't be replaced. I knew that it technically could be replaced, but the fact that it was the last thing my dad bought for me made it irreplaceable. I was relieved to see that my cupcake was untouched. However, my room was tossed as well, not as bad as my mother's though.

I turned around to find my mom right behind me, staring at the mess in my room. She shook her head while crying. I grabbed her hand, and we walk back to the dining room where my Uncle Glen and Mike were waiting. Mike flipped over two chairs for Mama and me to sit.

"Thanks" I said. He nodded his head.

We sat in silence while Uncle Glen was on the phone. I was not sure who he was talking to. By the time he finished his conversation, the police were just arriving. Two officers approached the door, and one knocked on the door frame since the door was still open.

"Ms. Taylor, can we come in?"

"Yea, come on in officers."

"Hello Ms. Taylor, I'm Officer Monroe, and this is my partner, Officer Ritter," he said as he nodded his head towards Officer Ritter. "We're here regarding a break in. Are you ok?" Officer Monroe continued.

"Yes, my daughter and I are fine. We weren't here when the break in occurred."

Officer Ritter turned to Uncle Glen. "Mr. Taylor, I take it you and your men cleared the house?"

"Yes, we did."

"Was there anyone on the premises when you arrived?"

"Nope, it was clear," Uncle Glen replied.

Officer Monroe spoke to my mom. "Ma'am, do you mind if we take a look around?"

"No, go ahead." The officers left to take in the mess around the house.

Uncle Glen worked closely with the police in the area. Uncle Glen and my dad went into business together fifteen years ago. They started a high-end security service. They provided home and business security systems, bodyguards, business guards, event guards and so on. My dad and Uncle Glen were skilled in five different fighting styles. You could only imagine their muscular physique. Everyone they hired had to go through intense training. Not only learning and mastering the different fighting techniques, but they also had to go through intense weaponries training as well. They were able to expand their company nationwide, with mostly high-profile cliental.

Now that my dad was gone, Uncle Glen ran the company by himself. Since I turned eighteen, Uncle Glen wanted me to be part owner, but I was not ready yet. My dad and Uncle Glen created a multimillion-dollar company but, looking at my family, you would never know. My family prided themselves on giving back to the community.

We didn't drive around in fancy cars or live in mansions. We didn't want to draw attention to ourselves. CeCe and I were raised to know the meaning of hard work. Our parents wanted us to work for what we wanted in life. I understood that, but I think CeCe was just starting to understand. I was grateful for the life I was given.

I got up and went into the kitchen to look for a glass. Just when I was about to give up, I found what seemed to be the only wine glass left in the back of one of the cabinets. I poured my mom a glass of red wine. When I went to give my mom a glass of wine, I noticed she had a blank look on her face, an unreadable expression. I handed her the glass, hoping the wine would calm her down.

"Thanks sweetie," she said as she looked at me and gave me a weak smile.

"No problem," I said while I pulled my chair next to her to try to comfort her. I held her hand and leaned my head on her shoulder. Uncle Glen opened his phone to make another call, then walked down the hall towards the officers. Mike was standing at the door with his arms crossed against his chest, still looking at the damage done to the inside of the house.

"Why are y'all so dressed up?" my mom asked.

"We were just coming from a black-tie event."

"Oh! I'm sorry my drama ruined your event," my mom said while twirling the wine in her glass.

"Brenda, stop it!" Uncle Glen said, his deep voice demanding attention. He walked back towards us in the dining room with the two officers behind him. "You're family, that's much more important than some event. Plus, it was a pleasure for me and work for Mike," he continued.

Officer Ritter approached my mom with a pencil and pad. "Ms. Taylor, did you notice if anything was taken?"

"No, I haven't gone through anything yet."

"This actually looks like a crime of passion. Do you have any idea who might have done this?"

"Donnie! I know it was Donnie."

"Do you have any proof? What makes you think Donnie did this?" Officer Ritter asked.

"No, I don't have any proof, but he's been acting out lately," my mom said after taking a sip of her wine.

"Does Donnie have a last name?" Officer Ritter asked as he wrote down notes.

"I believe his last name is Hensley."

"Can you give me a description of Donnie?"

"He's tall. Probably about six foot-four or six foot-five. His skin is a deep dark-brown color, and he has short dreadlocs but the sides of his head is shaved," my mom answered.

I noticed Uncle Glen writing down his description as well.

"Do you know where we can find him?" asked Officer Ritter.

"No, he never would tell me where he lives. He would always say he's from the area."

"Were the two of you in a relationship?" Officer Monroe asked.

"No. We went out a few times, but that's it. Everything was cool until last night. I told him not to come around me, my daughter or my house."

"Why did you tell him that?" Officer Ritter asked.

"He grabbed my daughter's arm yesterday, out of anger."

"Is that true?" Officer Monroe asked, looking at me.

I looked at Uncle Glen before I answered; I could see him clenching his jaws. I looked back at Officer Monroe.

"Yes."

"Can you tell me what happened?" Officer Monroe asked.

"Yes, I had plans to go out with my mom yesterday. The plans changed, and I ended up going to work. When I was walking out the door to leave for work, Donnie arrived. He grabbed my arm and jerked me forward a little, asking where I was going."

"And what did you do afterwards?" Officer Ritter asked.

"I yanked my arm back and told him it was none of his business."

"Have you seen him again afterwards?" asked Officer Monroe.

"My daughter has!" Uncle Glen cut in. "My daughter and Brielle work at Ami's Boutique together. She said he came into the store today upset and was looking for Brielle," Uncle Glen continued.

"Do you know around what time?"

"Around twelve-ish," replied Uncle Glen.

"We seen him today too!" I spoke up.

"When?" Officer Ritter inquired.

"This evening in Scottsdale. We went to some random shopping center to get our nails done. When we were leaving, we spotted him walking towards us from behind mom's truck."

"He looked horrible, and you could smell the liquor on his breath," Mama added.

"Did he try anything with you?" Uncle Glen asked, clenching his jaw again. I could tell he was getting angry.

"He tried to grab my arm. Brielle and I pinned him up against my truck. I had my elbow in his throat."

Uncle Glen smiled and nodded his head. "My girls!" he said.

"Did that seem to anger him?" Officer Monroe asked.

"No, it did the opposite. He smiled and said he was intrigued," my mom answered.

"Yeah, then he said this is not over yet," I added.

"Well... it does look like you may have a possible stalker on your hands. I suggest you head down to the police station and file for a restraining order. Meanwhile, we are going to try and locate this Donnie guy, see if we can get some answers," Officer Ritter said.

"Please don't hesitate to call us if he comes back," Office Monroe said as they turned around to walk out the door.

"Glen, I was going to call you about this tomorrow, but I need a sweep done on both the house and our vehicles." Glen nodded his head.

"Ay Glen, we got some boards at the office. If you want, I could go grab them, board up the windows. I'll grab the detector too, have the sweep done before we leave here tonight."

"My man! Thanks," Uncle Glen said as he threw his car keys to Mike.

"Alright! I'll be back in ten," Mike said as he caught the keys with one hand, then turned and walked out the door.

Uncle Glen walked into the living room and started to turn the furniture back into its upright position. I got up to help him.

"I think you and Brie should come stay with us for a while or at least tonight," he said to my mom.

"I'm not letting him run me out of my house Glen," my mom said as she snatched a bag from underneath the kitchen sink in the kitchen and started picking up big broken pieces of glass. "I don't scare that easily," she continued.

"I know you don't," Uncle Glen replied, turning over the coffee table while shaking his head. He let out a frustrated breath. "Brielle, you're welcome to come."

"That's okay, I don't want to leave Mama," I replied while putting the throw pillows back onto the couch.

"Brielle, I see you still remember those moves your dad taught you!" Uncle Glen said while smiling.

"Yea," I answered, now helping my mom pick up glass off the floor.

"You know we have a full gym at the office. That's were Ciera goes to work out. You should come by, so we can freshen up your techniques."

"I will, I'll let you know when."

"Brenda, I'm about to unmount this tv and sit it outside. The tv in your room is fine. Would you want me to take it out of your room and put in the living room?"

"That's fine. I have my laptop. I can use that when I'm in my room," my mom said while grabbing a broom to sweep up the remaining glass particles on the kitchen floor.

After getting the dining room back in order, I walked down the hallway, picking up all the broken picture frames. All the pictures were in good shape except for the last family portrait of me, my mom and my dad. My dad was torn out the picture. I just stared at the picture, noticing how incomplete my family looked without my dad. I hated that the picture was ruined, but it was weird how it resembled the way my family felt now. Incomplete.

The sound of hammering snapped me out of my thoughts. I knew Mike was boarding up the windows. I continued cleaning up the mess in the hallway. It took about two hours to get the house back in order. After finishing up my room, I made my way to the living room and found mama, Uncle Glen and Mike sitting on the couch. I took a seat next to mama, leaned back against the couch and took a deep breath. I didn't know how exhausted I was until now. My mom looked at me.

"Brielle, why don't you go ahead and get in the bed? We're pretty much done here," she said as she played in my braids.

"Did you find anything with the sweep?" I asked.

"Five cameras around the house and one GPS tracker on your mom's car," Mike answered.

"Your car was clean Brie. The camera was in the kitchen, living room, hallway, your mom's room, and her bathroom," Uncle Glen informed me.

"Ewe, your bathroom Mama?" She just shook her head. "When did he even have time to hide cameras around the house?" I asked.

"Who knows? I didn't leave him alone long enough to walk through my house yesterday. For all we know, he could have hidden them tonight. As for the GPS tracker, he had plenty of time. I never park in the garage," she answered while still playing in my hair.

"So, I'm guessing he knows the cops are looking for him now?" I questioned.

"Maybe so, but you let us worry about him. Go on to bed. You have work in the morning," my mom said.

"Where are you going to sleep?" I asked. She shrugged her shoulders.

"I don't know. Probably on this couch. I might see if I can have someone come clean and sanitize my mattress tomorrow."

"You can sleep in my bed. I'll sleep on the floor."

"No, that's ok, thanks for offering though," she said as she rubbed her temples.

"Like I said, you can always come stay with me," Uncle Glen said. My mom cut her eyes at him.

"Glen!"

"Alright! I'm just saying, the offer still stands," Uncle Glen said, holding up his hands as if he's surrendering. "You know one of the things Gerald loved about you the most was that you never ran from a problem, you always faced it head on," he continued.

My mom gave him a half smile. I had never seen my mom like this before. To say that I was amazed would be an understatement.

"Listen, Mike and I are about to head out." Uncle Glen stood up and stretched. "Tomorrow morning, I'm going to have someone come and install a security system for you. To be honest, I don't know why you don't have one already," he continued.

"Because I don't need one."

"Well. You need one now. Stop being so stubborn woman! There's a car outside. I got somebody to watch the house tonight."

"Glen! I don't need nobody watching my house. I'll be fine."

"Brenda, I love this whole, "Try me if you want to" attitude but, at the end of the day, you are my sister and that's my niece." Uncle Glen pointed at me. "Let me do my job and protect you. Your windows are boarded up, your house isn't fully secure. I'm not going home without my guys watching your house until them windows get fixed," he continued.

"Ok, fine," my mom said, sounding defeated. Uncle Glen walked over and kissed my mom and me on the cheek.

"Love y'all. Call me if you need me," he said as he and Mike walked out.

My mom got up to lock the door behind them and sat back down. I could see the tiredness in her eyes. I went get an extra pillow and blanket out the hallway closet and brought it to her.

"Thanks, Brie."

"Do you want me to sleep out here with you?"

"No, go on to bed. I'll see you in the morning."

"But it's already morning," I said with a smile.

"You know what I mean girl."

I smiled and kissed her on her cheeks. "Goodnight Mama."

11

Mmm... so good. I chewed slowly to savor the flavor explosion I was tasting. This barbeque turkey leg was the best. It really hit the spot. I had been munching on food all evening. I already had the deep-fried chicken in a cone, tacos, waffle cheese fries, and deep-fried Oreos. The best thing about the fair was the food and, right now, this turkey leg was heaven.

"Here you go Cupcake."

"My favorite! Thanks dad," I said as I took the bag of pink cotton candy from him and sat it on the table.

"I know you never leave a fair without it."

"Aw, are you saying it's time to go?" I whined.

"Well, Cupcake, we're going to have to leave eventually. The fair will be closing soon."

"Fine," I said with disappointment. "But, can we get on one more ride? Plus, I want to grab a deep-fried Snicker before we leave," I continued.

My dad laughed. "Why is it always a bargain with you to leave the fair? You've been doing this since you were five years old."

I shrugged my shoulders and continued munching on the turkey leg. "Can our last ride be the Ferris Wheel?"

"Sure, I think we have just enough tickets for that ride," he said as he counted our tickets.

"On our way out, can we get the deep-fried Snickers? I asked, knowing he would say yes.

"Didn't you have enough to eat Cupcake? You been eating since we got here."

"I only eat like this at the fair," I said as I tore the last piece of meat off my turkey leg. "And I only go to the fair once a year," I continued.

My dad picked up all my trash and threw it away. "The reason you only come once a year is because you eat like a pig when you're at the fair," he said.

I laughed. "Dad, that's because we only come once a year, and I love fair food. If you would bring me here more when they're in town, I wouldn't have to eat so much," I said, feeling insulted by his pig remark. My dad laughed and grabbed my cotton candy off the table. We started walking towards the Ferris Wheel.

"This is the first time we've come to the fair and you haven't eating anything," I said, noticing he didn't even try to taste any of my food. I normally had to run from him when I was trying different foods. He looked, at his watch.

"I'm not hungry, plus, you know I'm watching what I eat."

"If you say so. Mom says I get my pigging out from you." I looked at him curiously, as if he was hiding something.

After a five-minute walk, we finally reached the Ferris wheel. My dad handed our remaining tickets to the attendant. My dad stepped into the Ferris Wheel basket first, then me. After I sat, I closed the lap bar over us. We slowly went up until the rest of the baskets were filled. I noticed my dad looking at his watch again.

"Why do you keep looking at your watch? Do you have somewhere to be?"

"Naw, Cupcake. I'm right where I need to be. It's just crazy how fast time is moving."

"Yep, that's why they say time flies when you're having fun!" I replied. I noticed the ride was in full swing now. I took a breath and took in the moment. I loved the way the world looked at night when you were up in the air. All the lights were so mesmerizing. I looked over at my dad, and he was taking in the scenery as well. It was safe to say this was our favorite ride.

"You know Cupcake, I'm very proud of you. You have grown to be a beautiful and smart young woman. You're a great role model for Ciera. I know you girls are the same age, but she looks up to you."

I noticed the ride was coming to an end. We were halfway up when I noticed the first set of riders to exit the basket. That was the quickest five minutest ever. *Dad was right. Time is moving fast*, I thought to myself. I looked out into the world, taking in the beauty and enjoying the fact I got to go around one more time.

"You have a fire in you that I don't even think you know you have," my dad continued. "It's so funny how you look exactly like me, but you have your mom's personality." I smiled. We were almost to the very top of the Ferris Wheel.

"You remember when I was training you? I told you to always be observant, anticipate your opponent's move, that way you are always ready. These are skills you should be using every day. You hear me, Cupcake?"

"Yes, Daddy."

"Always be observant, don't ever let anyone blindside you," he said.

We finally reach the top of the Ferris Wheel. Both my dad and I took in the scenery. "I love you, Cupcake!" he said. I smiled.

"Woah!" I say out loud as I slid over to hug him. I was just noticing how slippery my leggings were over the seat. I gave him a tight embrace. "I love you too, Daddy!"

While hugging him, the ride did a hard jerk and I slid back, hitting the lap bar and popping it off the hinge. I fell out the basket backwards, staring into my dad's green eyes while I was screaming.

He looked down at me from the basket and whispered, "Pay attention," and I heard him as if he was in my ear.

I felt like I couldn't breathe as I was falling. I felt as though needles were pricking my arms and legs. Everything went dark. I forcibly took a deep breath and coughed. I couldn't stop coughing. I opened my eyes and all I saw was black smoke. There was smoke everywhere. I sat up and realized I was in my bed.

"Mama!" I yelled. No answer. I continued to cough as I got up, trying to tuck my nose inside the shirt I was wearing. I walked over to my door and put my hand near the doorknob to feel for heat. I opened the door without getting burned and looked down the hall. I could see the front of the house engulfed in flames.

"Mama!" I screamed, knowing she was sleeping in the living room. "Mama!" I cried out again.

I hurried to the bathroom across from me and grabbed a towel. I wet it and rung it out a little. I covered my nose with the wet towel, hoping it would help me to breathe a little better. I hurried down the hall to check my mom's room, praying that she was in there. I pushed her door open, trying my best to see in the thick black smoke.

"Mommy!" I yelled. My chest was burning; it was getting harder to breath. I tried staying low to the floor while trying to feel for her. I walked over to her window, noticing it was no longer boarded up. There was a full window in place of the board. I jumped when I hear the door slam close.

"Mom!" I called out. The visibility in the room was bad. It was getting harder to breathe. I walked against the wall to her ensuite. I stepped down onto the bathroom floor and slipped on something wet. I fell butt first and landed on my elbows.

"Watch your step... it's a little messy in here," he laughed.

"Donnie!" I screamed. My elbows were throbbing, but the adrenaline I was feeling masked the pain. "What are you doing here? Where is my mom?" I coughed.

"She's right next to you," he said. He spoke so clearly; it was as though the smoke wasn't even bothering him.

I looked down to the corner on my right and saw her lying face down on the floor. "Mom!" I screamed as I bent down to try to turn her over.

"Um… I wouldn't do that if I was you. She definitely doesn't look like the same woman. That was her blood you slipped on. I think one of her eyeballs rolled behind the toilet," he said as he bent down as if he was looking for it. I rolled her over and screamed.

"Mom!" I cried, rocking her back and forth in my arms. Her face was split wide open; her neck was deeply sliced.

"What did you do?" I screamed.

"The same thing I'm about to do to you," he said as he bent down to pick up a machete.

I got up as fast as I could and took off. When I reached the bedroom door, I could hear a loud thud. I knew he fell and dropped the machete. I reached for the doorknob and snatched it open, burning my hand in the process. The fire was so close to me; my skin was burning as I was running back to my room. I shut the door and locked it. I went to the window to open it. Donnie started banging on my door.

"If it makes you feel better, your mom never saw it coming!" he yelled from the other side of the door.

I noticed he still hadn't coughed. It was as though the fire and smoke didn't bother him. The window was jammed, and I couldn't push it back. I quickly tried my best to find out what was blocking the window while coughing and crying. My eyes were burning and it was getting so hard to breathe. Donnie continued talking while hacking away at the door.

"This is all your fault Brielle!" he screamed. "Your little lie caused your mom's death, and it's about to cause your death too. You have ruined my whole plan!" he screamed as he kicked the door down.

At this point, I gave up on the window. I was just sitting in a corner feeling like I was suffocating. It was so hard to breathe; my chest hurt. I was lying on the floor staring at the doorway, as Donnie entered the room. I was convinced Donnie was either the devil himself or just so filled with hate and anger towards me that the burn from the fire didn't bother him.

"I was supposed to bring happiness back into your lives, protect you from the hurt and loss after your father died. It was my job to take your father's place. He didn't deserve what he had. This house should have been mine!" he shouted. "Do you know how long it took me to get your mom to go out with me? Three years of hard work, ruined because of your lies! You have messed up a perfectly good plan. So, in return, I get to mess up your lives," Donnie said as he lifted the machete.

I closed my eyes, welcoming death, praying that it was quick so I could be with my mom and dad. I was too weak, too tired to continue to fight. The fight in me was gone. Everything was dark. I waited to feel the blade of the machete on my skin. My feet and hands were tingling from the lack of oxygen. I had this sensation that I was falling again. I gasped for air and opened my eyes. I was in my bed, everything looked normal.

"Mama!" I screamed out while crying. "Mama!" I cried out again. I tossed the covers back and hopped out the bed. I threw the door open to find my mom standing on the other side of the door. "Mama!" I cried as I dropped to my knees, hugging her. She fell to the floor with me.

"Brielle, what's wrong?"

"There was a fire, the house was on fire. Donnie was here! He killed you, Mama!" I sobbed uncontrollably, unsure if she was able to make out what I was saying. "He had a machete, he snuck up on you. He was after me. I was trapped in my room. I couldn't breathe. It was so much smoke." I was crying hysterically.

"Shh, baby, it was just a bad dream. We're ok. I'm here," she said, comforting me in a tight hug while rubbing my back.

"It seemed so real Mama!" I cried.

"Look at me, Brielle! It was just..."

"Ouch!" I yelled out after she touched my left hand. I looked down at my hand, and there was a doorknob print burned into my hand. My fingertips were burned. I looked at the side of my arm. It was burned also, some parts of my arm already starting to blister up.

"Oh, my God! Brielle, what happened?" she asked, shocked at the sight before her.

"It was a... fire," I said right before I passed out.

12

I woke up to Aunt Sherri and mama sitting at my bedside. They were talking about the break-in last night. They were so deep in conversation that they didn't know I was awake until I coughed.

"Brie! Are you okay sweetheart?" Aunty Sherri asked me.

"What happened?" I asked while trying to sit up. I was quickly reminded of what happened by the pain in my arm when trying to pull myself up.

"You fainted," my mom answered. I noticed my arm and hand was bandaged up.

"I came right over as soon as your mom called," Aunt Sherri said after noticing me looking at my bandages. "Thank God, I had today off. Those are second-degree burns Brie. What happened?" Aunt Sherri asked.

"Donnie is what happened," I replied while still looking at my bandages.

"What did he do?" Aunt Sherri asked, getting upset.

"He killed mama and set the house on fire. Maybe not in that order, but he was trying to kill me too. I was trapped in my room."

"It was just a dream," my mom said as she was trying to fluff up my pillows.

"Dreams don't hurt mama," I said, a little annoyed.

"Listen, you guys. I've been going through some things that are pretty unbelievable. But it can explain how I got these burns." My mom sat down in a chair at the head of my bed, facing me. She had a worried look on her face. Aunt Sherri sat at the foot of my bed with a curious look on her face.

"Well, it started when I was in Mississippi, when CeCe and I got lost. I went inside this abandoned shack... something happened, and I saw two slaves named Kitty and Frannie. They were having a..."

"Slaves?" my mom questioned me as if I had officially lost my mind.

"Yes, slaves! Just please listen to everything before you or Aunt Sherri question what I'm saying. I sort of have proof," I pleaded.

My mom nodded her head and took a deep breath. "Go ahead," she said, letting me continue my story.

"Kitty and Frannie were having a serious discussion about Kitty running away. I also heard the reason behind her wanting to leave." I sat up a little farther to reach for my nightstand drawer. I opened it and pulled out the booklet Aunt Gracie made. I turned to the page with the family tree and the letter written by Aunt Gracie. I handed it to mama. "I read this after I went back into the past. This booklet is how I found out that Kitty and Frannie were my third and fifth great grandmothers," I said, as mama started reading. Aunt Sherrie had a surprised look on her face.

"I don't know if I would necessarily call this proof Brie," Mom said as she handed the booklet to Aunt Sherri.

"I'm not done Mama."

"Did CeCe go in the shack with you?" Aunt Sherri asked, taking the booklet.

"No. She was asleep in the car." Aunt Sherri shook her head. "Mama, remember the day before yesterday, you and I was supposed to have our mother-daughter day, but I went to work instead. I got off work at six o'clock pm. When I came home, you was standing in the kitchen and Aunt Sherri was sitting at the bar drinking wine. I remember y'all was laughing so hard, you had tears. Mama, you were talking about telling someone off and then walking away with half your butt cheek showing."

Mama and Aunt Sherri stared at each other blankly. "Mama, I don't know if you remember me asking if you took my cucumber melon body spray. That day, I found my body spray under my bed, and I tossed it in my purse." I grabbed my purse from on top of the nightstand.

"How did you know you were in the past again?" mama asked me.

"I tried to talk to the both of you, and I was ignored. Then, I touched your skin, you were freezing. Then, Aunt Sherri said she was missing General Hospital. That's when I looked at the time. It was 1:25 p.m. When I came back to reality, I found this in my purse." I tossed them the cucumber melon body spray. I could tell Aunt Sherri was starting to believe me when she sucked in air.

"Brenda, how could she have known that? She wasn't there." Mom shrugged her shoulders.

"Well, obviously, she was. I never told her that story."

"Were there any other times?" Aunt Sherri asked.

"Yeah, last night. Last night was a little different though. I was with daddy at the fair." My mom rolled her eyes

"Brielle!"

"Mom. I know it sounds crazy, but it seemed so real. We laughed and rode rides. I ate so much. Actually, I thought it was a dream until now."

"Why now?" Aunt Sherri asked.

I pointed to my dresser. "Daddy surprised me with cotton candy after I finished eating." Mom grabbed the cotton candy and slowly passed it to Aunt Sherri.

"Mama, you and I hung out all day yesterday. Not once did we buy cotton candy. When we got home, the house was a mess. Not once did we see any cotton candy while we were cleaning up, and I'm pretty sure you checked on me throughout the night like you always do. I'm confident you didn't see any pink cotton candy on my dresser." I thought for a minute. "To be honest, I don't know how the cotton candy is here. Daddy was holding it the whole time."

"Wait! I'm confused," my mom said, rubbing her temples. She continued, "Why would you think spending time with your dad was a dream but not the other times that you went into the past?"

"Because I was awake for the other times. Plus, it was the way my visit with daddy ended."

"But this doesn't explain how you got burned," Aunty Sherri said.

"I'm getting to that. At the last moment that I was with daddy, I was falling from a Ferris Wheel. I started coughing mid-fall. When I opened my eyes, I was in bed and there was smoke everywhere. I couldn't breathe. At this point, I thought my time with daddy was a dream." My mom nodded her head in understanding.

I continued, "When I opened the door to my room, the whole front of the house was engulfed in flames. Last I remembered, mama, you were sleeping in the living room. I decided to go check your room just in case you went in there. Mama, I found you in your bathroom lying on the floor. Blood was everywhere." I started crying again at the memory of my mom lying there lifeless. My mom rubbed my back and Aunt Sherri rubbed my legs to comfort me.

"Donnie was standing in your bathroom with a machete. When he started to come after me, I opened your bedroom door." I held up my bandaged hand. "The fire was so close mama, it was basically at your bedroom. When I

236

ran into the hallway is when my arm got burned." The room went silent.

"So, what does all this mean?" my mom asked.

"I don't know mama," I sighed while leaning back against my pillow. "When I go back into the past, I get so caught up in the un-realness of it all that I don't pay attention to... oh, my God. Pay attention!" I yelled out as I sat up in bed.

"What?" my mom and Aunt Sherri said in unison.

"That's what daddy was telling me when I fell off the ride. When the ride started, Daddy was telling me how proud he is of me. He mentioned to use the skills he taught me every day. Be observant, anticipate my opponent's move and to always pay attention. He said, that way, I'll stay ready!"

"Okay. Well, clearly, Gerald is trying to help with this Donnie situation and, Brenda, you have got to admit this situation has gotten out of hand."

"Are you trying to tell me you believe all this?"

"And you don't? Brenda, come on. This girl is telling you things that was said between us while she was at work. She even knows what I said about my soap operas. I'm pretty sure she heard more of our conversation that day, right Brie?"

"You mean like how mama thought Donnie was too perfect and always available, and how she wasn't sure that was a red flag?" I replied. Aunt Sherri looked back at mama with a smirk.

"It would explain the burn," Aunt Sherri stated.

"Okay, okay! Brielle, why do you think this last experience was different than the others?" my mom asked.

I thought for a moment before answering, trying really heard to focus on what I saw and heard when the house was on fire. "There is one thing I noticed when the house was on fire. Mom, Mike boarded up the living room window and your bedroom windows, right?"

"Yeah."

"When I was in your room looking for you, there were no boards. The window had been replaced. I think I was in the future this time."

"Brenda. When are your windows being replaced?" Aunt Sherri asked.

"Tomorrow"

"Brie, did you see anything with a date on it?" Aunt Sherri asked.

"No. I couldn't really see anything. It was too smokey."

"Did Donnie say anything?" my mom asked.

"Yeah, he had a lot to say. He said that you died quick mama and that you didn't see it coming. When he was going after me, he said that I ruined his plan. That he was supposed to take away our hurt and pain away from losing daddy. He said he was supposed to take daddy's place."

"Why would he think you guys were hurting?" Aunt Sherri asked.

"I have no idea why he would think that. I never gave him a reason to."

Aunt Sherri turned to me. "What about you, Brielle?" she asked.

"No, I've never really talked to him."

"Well, I know he knows Gerald passed. Maybe he thinks you guys are still hurt from the loss," Aunt Sherri said while she got up from the bed and grabbed her phone off the dresser. "I'm about to call Glen, make sure the security company knows to put sensors on all windows and doors."

My mom sighed, "Is that really necessary?"

"If what Brielle saw is a glimpse of what's to come, then yes. Glen told me you were being difficult."

"I just don't like living like this. I got a car out front watching my house, cameras, motion lights, sensors being installed; this is too much!"

"Mom, we should also get security screen doors for the front and back door."

"No, that won't be necessary!" my mom responded while shaking her head.

"Actually, that's a good idea, I'll tell Glen." Aunt Sherri gave me a wink before walking out to make the call to Uncle Glen.

"Brielle!" my mom said to me, clearly annoyed.

"I'm sorry but, what I went through last night, I don't want to go through ever again," I said while looking at my bandages.

"Uh, I wish your dad was here!" my mom yelled out as she got up from her chair and went to stand next to the window, looking out.

"I do too Mama but, even if daddy was here, he would still want a security system in the house. You always fought him on that."

"That's why we moved to this area because it's nice, safe and quiet. We don't need all that stuff."

"Any area can be safe, nice and quiet. It's the people that bring the chaos."

"You sound like your father."

"Where you think I got it from?" I laughed. "What time is it?" I asked, throwing my legs over the side of my bed to get up.

"Twelve, noon."

"Oh no! I'm late" I said as I quickly jumped up from the bed and walked to the closet.

"Hold on Brie! You're not going anywhere. I called Ami and told her you were in an accident. You're not going anywhere except with me."

"Oh... okay. Thanks Mama," I said, relieved.

"She took you off for a few days," my mom said.

Aunt Sherri returned, standing in the doorway. "Okay ladies, I'm about to head out. Brenda, Glen said to tell you the car will remain out front until the security system is up and running. The technician will be here tomorrow morning between eight and ten. Also..." Aunt Sherri laughed, "you're going to love this part! Glen said he has somebody tailing you while you're out shopping today." Aunt Sherri smiled.

"No! No! No! That's where I draw the line. Glen already found the tracker on my truck. I don't need a bodyguard, Sherri!"

"First of all, Brenda. You can't draw and, secondly, better safe than sorry!" Aunt Sherri said before turning to me.

"This is ridiculous!" my mom yelled out while walking out my room.

"Brie, I left you a bag on the table; it's full of gauze rolls and antibacterial ointment. I want you to change the bandages once a day and make sure to apply the ointment all over the burn area with each change, okay."

"Yes, Aunt Sherri. Thank you."

"No problem. I'll be back to check on the healing process. I might even stop by tomorrow with Glen. Alright! I got to go. I'll catch y'all later, love you," she said as she disappeared into the hallway.

"Love you too!" I yelled out.

"Hey Sherri! Just to let you know, I'm ditching your bodyguard today!" Mom yelled out from her room.

"Girl, I'm not worried about you! You can't even ditch Donnie!" Aunt Sherri yelled back, right before the front door closed shut.

I shook my head as I walked into my mom's room to try to comfort her. "You okay, mama?"

"No, I'm not. I'm tired of everyone acting like I can't take care of myself. Donnie doesn't scare me. I can take him and his craziness!" my mom yelled out in anger as she walked into her ensuite and turned on her shower. I followed her to the doorway, looking at the floor where I saw her lifeless body. I shivered at the memory.

"Well, he scares me, Mama. There are so many people in this world going through the same thing we are, and they can only wish that they had the same resources we have."

"I get that but, like I said, I can take care of myself. I stay ready," she said as she stepped into the shower.

"Well, you weren't ready when I got these burns. You can't watch your back without exposing your front, therefore you are vulnerable Mama, no matter how much you stay ready."

"There you go sounding like your father again," my mom said, sounding more annoyed.

I laughed. "Mama, Uncle Glen knows you well. I'm sure he told whoever is tailing us to stay discreet."

"They better if they know what's best. Go get ready. I don't want to be gone all day. We have to replace everything Donnie broke."

"Isn't someone coming to clean the mattress today?" I asked.

"No, I decided to get a new one."

"That sucks, you just bought that one."

"I know, go get dressed Brielle. You're wasting time with all your questions," my mom said, turning the shower off.

"Alright, alright," I replied as I turned to go back to my room. I grabbed my phone off my dresser and sat on my bed. I noticed I had a missed call from Loyal. I quickly called him back. It rang a few times before he answered.

"Hello," he answered.

"Hey. Sorry, I missed your call."

"That's alright. I was calling to check on you. Ami asked me to work your shift. She said you had an accident. Are you ok?"

"Yeah, I'm ok. I'm all bandaged up. I have a second-degree burn on my arm and hand."

"Dang girl! What happened?"

"It's a long story. I'd rather not talk about it."

"No problem. I can respect that. Do you want to reschedule our date? It's ok if you want to," he asked, concerned. I thought it was nice that he cared about my well-being.

"No. We can still hang out. I'm good," I answered. Honestly, I did feel better knowing that I was able to share what I been going through with Aunt Sherri and Mama. I was not sure if Mama fully believed me, but I knew Aunt Sherri did. I felt like so much weight was lifted off my shoulders.

"Alright then, I'll pick you up at six p.m."

"I'll be waiting!" I said with a smile.

"Ha, well, I better get off this phone before Ami figures out I'm missing."

"Okay. See you later."

"Alright, later," he said before hanging up the phone.

"Aww, he was worried," I said to myself out loud as I leaned back in my bed while smiling, wondering what to wear for the day.

13

Besides the constant pain in my arm, today was a good day so far. After stopping by the police department to file for a restraining order, we headed to a department store that sold everything we needed, including mattresses. Mama wasn't playing when she said she didn't want to be shopping all day. Mama kept her guard up the whole time we were out, constantly looking around. I didn't know if she was keeping a lookout for Donnie or trying to see if she could spot our tail. Maybe even both. I would be lying if I said I wasn't regularly looking around as well. Other people probably thought we were acting suspicious, but nobody questioned us.

I could tell my mama was in a bad mood. There was no smile on her face, no conversation. It was just pure irritation and anger with every step she took and every word she spoke. She was a completely different person from yesterday. I didn't take it personal though. I understood her feelings. She felt her life was completely transparent right now, and my mama was a very private person. She was way out of her element.

I, on the other hand, felt safe but I also felt anxious about what's to come. I couldn't shake the memory of my mom's lifeless body lying on the floor. I tried my best not to think about it but, every time I looked at her, the image of her lifeless body popped in my head.

I leaned back in my seat, staring out the window and watching the world pass me by, lost in the quietness of the car. We were gone for about three hours before we finally arrived back home. After lugging all the bags into the house, I help Mama unload the dinnerware, picture frames and other little home decorations that were damaged from the break-in.

After helping Mama wash, dry and put the new dinnerware away, I decided to go take a nap. After the night I had, I was mentally and physically drained.

"Mama, I'm going to take a nap."

"Okay. Isn't your date with Loyal this evening?"

"Yeah. He'll be here at six p.m." I sighed.

"Oh, then you got some time! Where y'all going?"

I shrugged my shoulders. "I don't know, dinner, maybe a movie. We might go bowling. I haven't thought much about it," I said, leaning against the hallway wall. I was secretly irritated that she wanted to have a conversation now while I was so tired.

"How about y'all go to the fair? You always go at least once when the fair is in town. You haven't been yet," she said while taking picture frames out the bag.

"Really mama! I just went to the fair last night with daddy, remember," I said, shocked at my mom's suggestion.

"That was a dream Brielle."

"Mom! I thought you believed me! How do you explain the cotton candy?"

My mom said nothing. I watched her, as she continued taking items out the bag. Then, she walked around the island to throw the bags in the trash. I just shook my head. I refused to be upset just because she was upset.

"No Mama. I don't want to go to the fair," I said as I turned into the hallway. I knew my mom was just upset about our way of living right now and I was trying my best not to take her attitude personally. I closed the door to my room and threw myself on the bed. I didn't recall how long it took for my body to shut down. Before I knew it, I was out like a light.

I woke up to a phone call from CeCe. I stared at the phone for a moment before answering it, still waiting for my brain to wake up I guess. "Hello," I answered, trying not to sound like I just woke up.

"Hi Brie. My mom told me what happened. Are you okay?" asked CeCe.

Yeah. She bandaged me up pretty good."

"Dang! Second-degree burns Brielle! I'm sorry I didn't believe you about your... experiences? I don't even know what to call them."

"No problem. I'm just thankful somebody believes me." I exhaled. "So glad this isn't a burden I have to carry on my own anymore."

"Oh! Guess what I did?" CeCe said.

I could tell she was all smiles on the other end of the phone. "You got fired?" I answered sarcastically.

"Really Brie!"

"I'm just playing," I laughed. "Well, what is it? You know I hate playing the guessing game."

"I registered for classes!" she blurted out.

"Wait! Did you just say classes? As in more than one."

"Yep. I decided to major in Kinesiology."

"Wow! That's great CeCe. Congrats on finding out what you want to major in," I said with more excitement in my voice. I was happy for CeCe. She must have really needed that talk we had.

"Thanks. I'm going to be taking a full load."

"A full-time student and a part-time employee. I know your parents are happy."

"Yeah, they are, but my dad makes sure to remind me that you and I are supposed to take over the business one day."

"I know. He's been hinting for me to take my dad's place, but I'm not ready yet. I'm still young. I want to try my own thing first. How's work going?"

"Work is good. I'm getting the hang of things. Sucks I haven't worked with you yet."

"You'll get a chance to." I sat up to glance at the clock on my dresser, surprised that it's almost six o'clock. I needed to end this conversation soon. "Speaking of work, I have to go. I'm going on a date with Loyal."

"Loyal? I know him, he's cute! I didn't know you guys were dating."

"I know, I've been crushing on him for months, so he's off limits."

"Calm down! I'm not eyeing your dude. I got my eyes set on someone else."

"Who?" I asked, shocked that this was my first time hearing about this.

"You don't know him. I met him at the gym."

"So, that means your dad knows him?" I gloated. Uncle Glen was very tough with the guys CeCe and I brought around. With his mind being on CeCe's crush, maybe he wouldn't give Loyal such a hard time.

"Yeah, unfortunately. That means he already created a profile on him. That's why I'm not going to tell him until we've been out a few times."

"Ooh! Your dad is going to get you," I teased.

"Whatever. I'm twenty-one years old. He can't tell me who I can and can't date." I could tell CeCe was getting irritated with this conversation.

"No. You're right. He can't, but they can go missing."

"Yeah and so can Loyal."

"But the difference is Uncle Glen doesn't know Loyal. He has to get to know him. He already knows... what's his name?" I asked

"Brayden."

"He already knows if he likes Brayden and if he would allow him to date you. If your dad can't tell you who to date, then why wait to tell him about Brayden?" I asked. I honestly wanted her to tell him, so he wouldn't be too worried about Loyal.

"Because I don't feel like arguing with that man!" she yelled. I knew she was getting frustrated. We learned early to avoid conversation with Uncle Glen regarding boys. Yes, he was my Uncle, but he was just as hard on me and my dates as he was on CeCe. I started feeling bad trying to push CeCe to come clean for my own selfish reasons. After all, I had no plans on telling him about Loyal either.

"Just make sure to tell your mom about him first, so she can have your back when you decide to tell Uncle Glen about him," I said, ready to end this conversation. "I have to go. Loyal will be here in ten minutes and I'm not even dressed yet."

"Okay. Let me know how your date goes."

"I will. Talk to you later!"

"Bye!" CeCe said.

I pressed the end button on the phone, tossed it on the bed and hopped up to go take a shower. I was careful not to get the bandages wet. After my shower, I quickly dried off and ran to my room to lotion up. The whole time,

I was trying to think of something cute yet comfortable to wear on my date with Loyal. I settled on some light-blue skinny jeans and a white half-button spaghetti crop top. I stood in front of the full-bodied mirror hanging on the inside of my closet door. I hated the way the bandages on my arm and hand stood out with every outfit I tried on. I decided to throw on my tan knit cardigan and slid on my tan studded sandals to match. I tied my hair up in a half-bun, half-down style. The only thing missing was my silver heart pendant necklace and my silver dangle earrings.

Once I was satisfied with my look, I spritzed on some of my cucumber melon body spray. I looked at the time, and it was six-fifteen and Loyal wasn't there yet. I called him to see if he was lost. The phone rang once before he answered.

"What's up Brielle! How are you feeling?" He sounded like he was concerned but happy I called. His greeting had me a little confused.

"I'm okay... did you get lost?"

"No. I was going to call you when I got home. We could have rescheduled if you weren't feeling good. I know you're hurt."

"What are you talking about? I feel fine. I'm all dressed and waiting on you."

"Your dad said you were in pain and didn't want any company. He said you took some medication that had you knocked out for the past hour." Now, Loyal sounded confused.

"That's impossible! My dad died three years ago," I said slowly. Loyal went quiet for a moment. All I could hear was the sound of his car.

"I clearly talked to someone, Brielle. He said your name."

"How did he look?" I asked.

"Shiny bald head, clean shaven, tall guy."

I quietly sucked in a breath. Donnie had changed his appearance and was still sneaking around watching us. "That wasn't my dad."

"Well, then, who was he? He was walking in front of your house when I walked up."

"Can I tell you when you get here? I mean if you don't have other plans already."

"I'm on my way."

"Okay. Call me when you get here."

"Alright. See you in soon," he said before hanging up. I immediately called Uncle Glen. He also answered on the first ring.

"Everything okay Brielle?"

"Yeah. I'm fine... but Donnie changed his appearance."

"How do you know? Did you see him?"

"No, I didn't. My date did when he came to get me. He said Donnie approached him as my father. Told him I was in too much pain for company and that I took some meds that knocked me out."

"Wait! You have a date? With whom?"

I palmed my forehead, wishing I would have said anything else other than having a date. "Yes, you don't know him. His name is Loyal."

"You are going on some date with a cat named Loyal and I don't know about it?" he yelled into the phone.

"My mom knows!"

"As she should, but I need to know these things too. Your dad ain't here anymore, so it's my job to grill these lil dudes you be bringing around here, you understand!" he said, still raising his voice.

"Yes, Uncle Glen," I said, feeling defeated.

"And another thing. Whenever you decide you need to leave the house, you need to let me know, so I can put a tail on you until this whole Donnie situation blows over... are you hearing me, Brielle?"

"Yes, Uncle Glen."

"So, where y'all supposed to be going on this date?" he asked, calming down.

"I'm not sure yet."

"You're not sure!" he yelled again. "How is he taking you on a date and you don't know where y'all are going? I'm already not liking this guy."

"It's my decision on where we were going tonight. I haven't made up my mind yet."

"Well, don't you go anywhere without telling me where, so I can put a tail on you, you hear me?"

"Yes, Uncle Glen," I said, literally biting my tongue.

"Alright, let me go, so I can update my guys on Donnie."

"Okay, bye," I said and hung up before he could respond. "Ughh!" I screamed out. Why did he have to treat me like I was still in high school? "I'm twenty-one years old and I'm not even his daughter!" I yelled out loud.

Now, I understood why CeCe wouldn't tell him about Brayden. Uncle Glen could be very intimidating. There was no winning arguments with him unless your name was Sherri. She was the only person that could really calm his beast down enough to get him to think about his actions. Not even my mama could win a fight with Uncle Glen. Both could be very stubborn though. I tried my best to put my anger aside. I didn't want to be in a bad mood when Loyal arrived.

I got up to go check on mama. I peeked in her room and found her sleeping, so I decided to go wait for Loyal in the living room.

"You still here?" she asked, startling me.

"Mom!" I jumped. "You scared me. I thought you were sleeping."

"Nope, just resting my eyes" she said with her eyes still closed.

"I see Loyal isn't living up to his name. I thought you'd be gone by now."

"Wait! Mama, why are you laying on the bed? Donnie peed on it," I asked, frowning up my face. I noticed her bed was made up with a rose gold comforter, and pillows were positioned at the head of the bed.

"I put a mattress topper on it. That couch does nothing for my back."

"Oh," I replied as I walked over to sit on the foot of her bed. Mama's room looked normal except for the boards over her double window, and her bed bench was gone. Daddy's dresser was back up in its original position. We threw away all his damaged clothes. The only clothes of his that was still in good condition were the ones hanging in the closet. Mama talked about donating those, eventually.

"So, what happened? You're not going out?"

"Donnie happened again."

"What? What he do now?" my mom asked, opening her eyes to look at me.

"Loyal was here. Donnie approached him as he was walking up to the house. Donnie introduced himself as my father and told Loyal that I was in too much pain to go out.

Donnie said that I had taken some mediation and went to sleep. So, Loyal left."

"How was Donnie even able to approach him with Glen's people watching the house? They don't need to be here if they can't do their job," my mom said, getting upset.

"Donnie changed his appearance. He's bald now, clean shaven," I said as I looked at my mom. She just shook her head and stared at the ceiling. I could tell my mom was frustrated.

"This game he's playing is getting old. I want my life back. Did you tell Glen?"

"Yeah, I called him. Then, he chewed me out," I said while lying back on her bed, staring at the ceiling myself.

"Is that what all the commotion was I heard? What he chew you out about?"

269

"For having a date and not telling him about it."

"That's understandable," she said, closing her eyes again.

"But I told you. You're my mom!" I said, getting upset that she wasn't on my side.

"Brielle, calm down and watch the tone in your voice!" my mother warned, looking at me. "Glen is your father's brother. It's only natural that he feels like it's his responsibility to watch over you. You are all he has left of your dad. Don't forget he's also your Godfather."

"Well, that still doesn't give him the right to treat me like a child." My mom said nothing. I remained quiet, pondering on what she said about me being all Uncle Glen had left of his brother. My phone vibrated, startling me out of my thought. A text message popped up from Loyal.

"Mama. I'll be back. Loyal is here."

"Um hum," she hummed with her eyes closed.

I rushed to the front door, opening it while telling myself not to seem too desperate. As soon as I opened the door, I spotted his navy-blue Ford Mustang parked across the street from my house. He was walking towards me wearing black shoes, dark blue jeans and a black muscle short sleeve top. My eyes grew big noticing for the first time how muscular he was. The outfits he wore to work did good hiding his muscles, or was I so mesmerized by how handsome he was that I just never noticed? I met him at the sidewalk. He greeted me with a big embrace. I inhaled deeply, loving the scent of his cologne.

"Hey beautiful!" he said with a smile on his face. I was shocked when he kissed me on my check. "Damn, hold up! I got something for you," he said as he ran back towards his car. There was a black SUV parked near me. I waved to the man inside, and he nodded his head. Loyal returned to me with a box of chocolates and some roses.

"Wow! Thanks," I said, as he handed me the gifts. I grabbed his hand and turned to walk back towards the house when he stopped me.

"Wait... you gone tell me who he was?"

"Dang, you waste no time," I said.

"Not when it comes to you. I've wasted enough time already," he replied. I couldn't help but to smile.

"So, basically, he's my mom's friend turned stalker. He's upset with me because I told my mom that he grabbed me up and now—"

"What do you mean he grabbed you up!" he asked, cutting me off. I could tell he really didn't like that last part.

"I'm good. It happened days ago."

"I wish I would have known that when I saw him earlier. Sorry for cutting you off. Finish what you were saying."

"Now, he's mad at me and my mom because she choose not to talk to him anymore." Loyal looked up at the house.

"What happened?"

"The same guy broke into the house last night while we were out," I answered. Loyal nodded his head.

"Sorry for all the drama," I said while looking down. I was embarrassed having to admit to everything. I didn't blame him if he wanted to walk away from me. Why couldn't we have started dating before my trip to Mississippi?

"Don't apologize! This isn't your fault. What... you think this guy is going to scare me away?" he asked while lifting up my chin. I smiled and grabbed his hand to lead him into the house. He looked around, nodding his head in approval.

"You have a nice house."

"Thanks," I said, closing the door behind us. Still holding his hand, I led him to the living room, and we had a seat on the sofa.

"So, you decide where you want to go?" he asked.

"No, not yet."

"You worried about that guy showing up while we're out?"

I shrugged my shoulders, knowing that it wouldn't be the first time he popped up somewhere out of the blue. Honestly, I really didn't feel like going out. I did until I found out that Donnie was still lurking around. Plus, I didn't feel like sneaking away to call Uncle Glen or coming up with a reason not to leave right away because we had to wait for a tail. I really didn't want to tell Loyal that we had somebody watching the house or that I needed a bodyguard every time I left the house.

"Do you mind if we just stay here? Maybe have a movie night?" I asked.

"That's fine with me. You have Netflix?"

"Yeah," I answered.

"Oh. Then, we're good! They been coming out with some good movies lately. You hungry?" he asked.

"Yeah, I can't remember the last time I ate. You thirsty?" I asked as I got up to go into the kitchen.

"Sure. I'll take whatever you have," he said, leaning back on the couch. I grabbed two glasses and grabbed the lemonade out the fridge. After pouring our glasses, I stared in the fridge, looking at everything inside.

"Hey, we have all we need to make tacos! How about tacos and movies?"

"That sounds good," Loyal said, getting up from the couch and meeting me in the kitchen. I handed him his glass; he took it and kissed me on the cheek.

"So, we're cooking together on our first date?" he said, taking a sip.

"If you're okay with that," I said, smiling.

"Yeah! It'll be fun. I love cooking."

"Really! I would have never guessed you to be the cooking type."

Loyal laughed while taking another sip of lemonade from his glass. "Everyone says that about me. I'm majoring in culinary arts and business. I want to be a chef someday, but I also want to open my own restaurant."

"That's good!" I said as I pulled out all the ingredients we needed for our tacos.

"Where do you keep the pots and pans?"

"It's the cabinet under the stove top," I pointed out. Loyal pulled out a skillet for the meat and to fry the shells.

"You have a cutting board?" he asked.

"Yeah. It's in the cabinet to the side." I pointed to a different cabinet as I pulled out the knives and cooking utensils. I kind of just sat back and watched how Loyal moved around in the kitchen. He was so comfortable with his surroundings. I normally felt weird cooking at other people's houses, especially if I was a first-time guest. I could tell Loyal was in his element. He moved so gracefully around the kitchen.

"Where do you keep your seasonings?"

"In the small cabinet right next to you."

"Ahh!" he said, finding the cabinet. "You got some good stuff in here," he said as he was looking through the seasonings. I didn't want him to catch me staring at him, so I started dicing onions.

"You know, I was going to cook for us. I didn't expect you to help."

"It's all good. I told you I love cooking... so you have any siblings?"

"Nope. Just me and my mom. She's in the back sleeping. What about you?"

"Two sisters and one brother."

"Are you the oldest?" I asked.

"No, I'm the youngest."

"Oh God! That means you're either spoiled because you're the baby of the family or you get away with everything. Which one is it?" I laughed.

278

"Well, I'm definitely not spoiled. All the spoiling went towards my sisters. However, I did get away with a lot growing up," he laughed as if he was thinking back to his childhood.

"I bet you guys had a lot of fun growing up," I replied.

"Yeah. We did. Did you ever want any siblings, or did you enjoy being the only child?"

"It never bothered me much. I grew up with my cousin, Ciera. We're the same age. I guess between the both of us, our parents felt we were enough," I said, shrugging my shoulders.

"Wait! Ciera! From Ami's? The new hire?" he asked, shocked at the news.

"Yep. That's her," I confessed.

"Wow, she seems cool. I should have known by her last name. Do you want kids?" he asked.

"Yeah, two. A boy and girl hopefully. What about you? Do you want kids?"

"Absolutely! I can't wait to be a father. I mean, hopefully, I have my career started before then."

"How many kids do you want?" I asked.

"It doesn't matter. As long as it's more than one," he said while stirring the meat.

"Are you and your siblings close?"

"Oh yeah! Family means everything to me." I nodded my head to his response as I fanned my eyes with my hands. I walked away from the onions.

"Your eyes burn?"

"Yes... I hate cutting onions."

"There's a trick to that. Next time, cut a lemon in half and rub it on the cutting board before you start cutting onions."

"Does that really work?"

"Yep, I do it all the time," he answered.

"I'll have to remember that. This is enough onions anyway," I said as I put the onions aside and covered it up to keep my eyes from burning more. I pulled out the cheese grater.

"I'll start grating the cheese," I said as I opened the cheese wrapper.

"The meat is almost done. I'll let it cook a little longer while I do the shells and dice up the tomatoes."

"What y'all doing in here? Got my house smelling so good!" Mama asked, coming from the hallway.

281

"Hey mama," I said. Loyal wiped his hands on a paper towel and introduced himself before I could do it.

"Hello Ms. Taylor, I'm Loyal," he said, holding out his hand.

"Hi Loyal. It's nice to finally meet you," Mama replied, shaking his hand.

"We decided to stay in and make some tacos. We're having movie night," I said.

"You're welcome to join us," Loyal added. I wasn't surprised at his offer. After all, he said he was big on family.

"No. I don't want to intrude, but I would like some of those tacos."

"There's plenty to go around." Loyal smiled.

After dinner was done, we all sat down at the table talking and laughing, getting to know one another. I could tell Mama was really enjoying herself. It was nice to see her smile for the first time today.

"Loyal, these were the best tacos I've ever had," my mom said as she pushed her chair back to get up from the table.

"Thanks!"

"You're going to make a great chef," she said as she got up to put her plate away.

"I got it Mama. I'm about to clean the kitchen anyway," I said, grabbing the plate from her.

"Thanks sweetheart. Well, I'm about to go back to my room and leave y'all to your movie." She turned to Loyal. "Loyal, it was nice meeting you again and I hope to see more of you."

"You definitely will," he said, getting up with his plate and helping me clear the table.

"Brie, there's popcorn in the kitchen. I just bought it. You're welcome to have it for your movie night."

"Thanks Mama, but I doubt we'll eat it. I'm stuffed. What about you, Loyal?" I asked.

"Yeah, me too. Them tacos hit the spot." He grinned while patting his stomach.

"Ok, well, goodnight you two."

"Goodnight," Loyal and I said in unison.

"So, what type of movies do you like?" I asked, as we made our way back to the living room. We finished cleaning up the kitchen and put the leftover food away.

"Action, comedy, drama?" he answered, as I took a seat next to him on the sofa.

"What about horror?" I asked.

"I can watch it. I'm not crazy about it though."

"Me too. I can do without it. Here… you can choose the movie," I said, handing him the remote.

"Alright! Let's see what's good," he said as he took the remote from me. I sat back on the couch, leaning against him as he put his arm around me. He picked the movie *It*.

"I thought you said you can do without scary movies?"

"I can. I just want to make sure you stay close to me," he said playfully.

"Loyal!" I blushed, hitting him in his chest. He kissed my forehead while laughing.

"I'm just playing, we're not watching this," he said, flipping through more movies. He ended up settling for *21 Bridges*. After that movie was over, I picked the second movie, *Morbius*.

"*Morbius*! Isn't that too scary for you?" Loyal asked.

"No. I actually like vampire movies."

"Vampires?"

"Yeah. Werewolves too," I replied with a smile. He shrugged his shoulders.

About thirty minutes into the movie, I started getting sleepy. I laid down on the couch. All I could remember was Loyal putting my feet on his lap and him giving me the best foot massage ever.

It felt like I had just closed my eyes when he woke me up to tell me he was leaving.

"So soon? The movie just started," I said, sitting up. Loyal laughed.

"Girl, the movie is over. You left me hanging about thirty minutes into the movie," he said, still rubbing my feet.

"It's your fault. Good food and a foot massage. What did you think would happen?"

"Then, I would say we did good on our first date," he said, still laid back on the couch. I could tell he was tired too.

"What time is it?" I asked, stretching.

"It's just after one in the morning," he answered, getting up.

"Sorry for falling asleep on you."

"That's alright, but we are going to have to work on your snoring."

"Wait, what? I don't snore," I said, embarrassed.

"I'm just playing with you, girl," he laughed as he got up to leave. "I had fun."

"Me too," I said, getting up to walk him to the door.

"Good! Listen, I work tomorrow morning… or should I say this morning. I'll call you afterwards, maybe I'll come thru if you're not busy."

"I'd like that."

"Alright!" he said as he pulled me in for a hug and gave me a passionate kiss before walking out.

"Call me when you get home."

Loyal laughed. "I'm sure you'll be asleep. I'll text you," he said, walking out the door.

"Okay. Be careful," I said as I closed the door and locked it.

I turned off the tv and walked to my room with a big smile on my face. I couldn't believe I spent the evening with Loyal. The fact that we were so comfortable around each other was weird to me. I touched my lips, reliving the kiss he surprised me with before walking out. I was surprised to learn how affectionate Loyal was. I always took him for the quiet, shy type. I laid back on my bed smiling, replaying the evening in my head as I fell asleep.

14

The sound of the doorbell woke me up. I could hear my mom coming out her room to answer the door. She had music playing, so I knew she must be in a good mood. I got out the bed and stretched. It was almost ten in the morning, so I didn't sleep in too late. I picked up my phone to see if Loyal texted me, letting me know he made it home safely. I shook my head, remembering him saying I'd be sleep by the time he got home.

Surprisingly, he did text me, and I replied to his message, telling him goodnight. I smiled, knowing that I proved him wrong. I was so tired after he left last night, I didn't even remember texting him back. A knock at the door caused me to look up.

"Hey Brie! How was your date?" my mom asked.

"It was fun." I smiled.

"He seems like a nice guy. I like him. Especially the fact that he can cook because you're going to need all the help you can get in that department," she laughed.

"Mom! I can cook."

"Ok. If you say so. I just wanted to let you know that workers are here to replace the windows, so don't be running across the hall naked after you take your shower." I couldn't help but to laugh.

"I never run across the hall naked Mama. What are you talking about?" I said as I gathered my things to take a shower.

"I be seeing you run across the hall after taking your showers."

"I don't be naked Mama. I always have a towel wrapped around me."

"Well, make sure it's not a brown towel," she said as she walked away. I just shook my head at her while going to get a pink towel out the hallway cabinet. I decided to take a cold shower since it was already hot outside.

The cool water hitting my skin felt amazing. I just stood underneath the shower head, taking relaxing breaths and trying to clear my head. I didn't realize how long I was in the shower until my mom knocked on the door, interrupting my meditation.

"Brie, hurry up! You have my water running too long!" she yelled from the door.

"Sorry! I'll be out in a minute!" I yelled back. I quickly lathered up, rinsed and turned the water off. I dried off completely before stepping out the shower and wrapped myself with my fresh pink towel. I quickly brushed my teeth and washed my face. I cracked the door open to peek down the hallway. I could see the workers working on part of the living room window. While their backs were turned towards me, I ran across the hall into my room.

I decided to wear my short, yellow spaghetti-strap sundress. I put my braids in a high bun and clipped in a yellow flower. I removed the wet bandages from my arm, looking at my burn for the first time. I had blisters of different sizes up and down my arm. Some of my skin was missing from parts of my arm. The biggest blister was on the palm of my hand. My burn didn't hurt as much until I took off the bandages. I wanted to hurry and bandage it back up, maybe it would the edge off some of the pain I was feeling. I walked into the living room to see my mom sitting at the table with Aunt Sherri. Uncle Glen was at the door talking to the technician that was to install the security system.

"Hi Aunt Sherri. Hey Uncle Glen!" I said as I walked towards the dining room table. Uncle Glen looked at me and nodded his head.

"Hey Brie! Come over here. Let me see that arm and bring that bag that I left you with medical supplies," Aunt Sherri said. I grabbed the bag off the counter and handed it to Aunt Sherri as I sat down next to her.

"I didn't know everybody was coming over so early," I said, looking around.

"You know your uncle. He made sure you all were first on everybody's route today," Aunt Sherri replied.

"Thank God because the sooner it's done, the sooner I can get my privacy back," my mom responded.

"Where's CeCe?" I asked.

"At the gym. Then, off to work in a couple of hours. I'm still not use to saying that. My baby is working," Aunt Sherri laughed.

"How's it looking?" I asked Aunt Sherri, as she examined my arm and hand.

"Still swollen, which is to be expected. The blisters are a normal reaction. You want to make sure not to pop the blisters. That would increase your risk of getting an infection. Are you in pain?"

"Yea. It didn't start hurting until after my shower when I removed the bandages," I said through the pain.

"Here, take these." She handed me a bottle of Ibuprofen. She started putting ointment all over the burn area and wrapped it back up with gauze.

"So... your mom tells me you went on a date last night," she said with a smile as she continued to roll the gauze around my arm. I glanced over at Uncle Glen. He looked at me with a raised eyebrow.

"Yeah. I had a date, but we didn't go anywhere. We stayed here."

"Girl, that boy can cook!" my mom said, bragging to Aunt Sherri.

"You had him cooking for you on your first date! Go ahead girl!" Aunty Sherri said, smacking my good shoulder.

"Well, we cooked together and had movie night. I didn't feel like going out but yeah. His tacos were fire! He wants to be a chef and open his own restaurant," I said, trying not to look at Uncle Glen. I didn't know if he was looking at me, but I knew he was listening.

"I can't wait to meet him," Aunt Sherri beamed.

"Neither can I," Uncle Glen added while walking towards the table.

"Why? So, you can scare him away?" I said sarcastically but honestly.

"That's my job," he replied with a serious look on his face.

Aunt Sherri smacked Uncle Glen on his leg. "Glen, stop! That's why none of the girls talk to you."

"I should have had me some sons. Help me scare these cats away."

"Yeah, well, you didn't so get over it," Aunt Sherri responded as she finished bandaging up my hand and arm.

Mama shook her head while laughing. "Glen, you always talking about the sons you don't have. If you stop scaring away these guys, maybe you'll get you some sons-in-law. Maybe even some grandsons," Mama said.

"I just don't want none of these ignorant dudes out here trying to put the moves on my girls. You better let me know the next time he comes over!" Uncle Glen said, looking at me.

"Leave her alone Glen! The girls are twenty-one years old. They're grown now. Both Ciera and Brie can pretty much date anyone they want," my mom said in my defense.

"Not if I can help it," Uncle Glen said with a serious expression. It was hard to tell when he was serious or being sarcastic.

"Don't listen to him, Brie!" my aunt said.

"Yo, since we all here, there's something I want to talk to you about." The doorbell rang, interrupting what Uncle Glen was trying to tell us.

"Brie, can you get the door for me? I ordered us some breakfast from the Breakfast Shack," my mom said as she walked into the kitchen, pulling out drinking glasses for everybody.

"Sure," I said as I got up and opened the front door to find nobody there. My chest felt heavy as I took a deep breath. My foot and hands were starting to tingle. Without panicking this time, I realized what was happening. My dad's voice played in my mind.

"Pay attention."

That's exactly what I planned to do this time, pay attention to what was being shown to me. I looked around. All the service cars that were parked out front were no longer there. Something about this day seemed familiar. It was the way the sun was shining. The warmth of the sun hitting my skin. The slight breeze in the air. Then, the sound of crushing metal made me snap my head towards the main road. My heart sank when I saw smoke and heard a horn honking continuously.

I started walking to the corner of the block with tears starting to fall down my cheeks. *Tell me it's not true!*

Tell me that I'm not reliving the worst day of my life again, I thought to myself. I was so caught up in my feelings that I didn't recognize the moment I ran past myself followed by my mom. I reached the intersection while wiping the steady stream of tears from my face. I tried my best to pay attention to my surroundings. This was just as hard for me as it was on the day that this happened.

I finally reached the intersection. I saw Mama holding me back on the sidewalk. I walked up to the car this time around, crying uncontrollably. I noticed my dad had his seatbelt on. It must have failed because he was leaning against the steering wheel. His eyes were open. There was blood coming from his nose and ears. The left side of his face was cut up from the broken window. I could see pieces of glass sticking out from the side of his face. The force of the big rig hitting the driver's side had my dad pinned in between the twisted metal of the car and the center console. The firefighters were definitely going to have to use the jaws of life to get him out. My dad's car had spun out from the impact. It landed away from the big rig and rested in the direction of impact. I couldn't stop the tears from coming down my face, no matter how hard I tried.

I was telling myself over and over that this happened three years ago, but it wasn't helping. I wanted so badly to go over to my mom and hug her for comfort, but I knew that would only depress me more remembering how cold her skin was the last time I touched her when I went back into the past.

I looked at the big rig that hit my dad's car. There was hardly any damage done. The door opened, and the driver slowly stepped down from the truck. My mouth dropped open. I inhaled and forgot to breathe. I wiped the tears from my eyes to make sure my eyes were not playing tricks on me. I couldn't believe it.

301

Donnie stepped away from the truck with a busted lip. He walked to my dad's car and looked at him. He stared at him for a moment; then, I noticed a brief smirk on his face. He looked over at my mom and me for a bit before putting both his hands on his head and stumbling over to the curb near his truck. He sat down and started to moan as if he was hurt.

My sorrows instantly turned to anger. My dad was murdered; this was no accident. He was taken from us by the hands of Donnie. I took a few steps backwards in disbelief. I closed my eyes and took a deep, slow breath.

When I opened my eyes, I was standing at my front door. The food delivery guy was leaving. I looked down and saw three bags of food on the ground. I bent down to pick it up, not knowing I was still crying until I saw the tear drops fall from my cheek and land on the bag.

I slowly brought the food to the table. I looked at my mom, aunt and uncle. My mom and Aunt Sherri were talking but stopped once they saw my face. Uncle Glen was messing on his tablet and had folders lying on the table in front of him.

"You okay Brie?" my mom asked. I shook my head no.

"He was murdered!" I said with a broken voice. My mom and Aunt Sherri had a confused look on their faces. Uncle Glen looked up from his tablet.

"Who was murdered?" Aunt Sherri asked.

"Daddy. It was no accident. Donnie was driving the truck that hit daddy," I said, trying to regulate my breathing from crying so hard.

"How do you know that?" Uncle Glen asked.

"Did it happen again?" asked Aunt Sherri.

I nodded my head yes. "Just now, when I opened the door to get the food." I looked over at Mama. She had a blank look on her face. Her emotion was unreadable at the moment.

"What happened again? What are you talking about?" Uncle Glen asked, clearly confused, looking at each of us.

"I've been having these experiences where I have been going back into the past and one where I was possibly in the future. It's as if someone is trying to show me something."

"That's how she got that burn on her arm," Aunt Sherri said.

"Wait! So, you're actually getting hurt when you have these so-called experiences?" he asked.

"No. This happened when I may have been in the future," I said as I lifted my bandaged arm.

"In the future! What happens in the future that causes you to get burned?"

"Donnie sets the house on fire... and killed mama with a machete."

"A machete!" Uncle Glen yelled out.

"I know it sounds crazy Glen, but she some-what has proo—"

"It does sound crazy, but I believe you!" Uncle Glen said, interrupting Mama. I was shocked when my mom spoke. This whole time, I didn't think she believed me.

"You believe me?" I asked Uncle Glen.

"Yeah. That's part of the reason I'm here. I wanted to go over some things that I found." He handed us each a printout of a job application for Mason Reed.

"What's this?" Aunt Sherri asked.

"Glen, this is not the time for us to consult on a possible candidate for employment," my mom sighed.

"Give me a sec," Uncle Glen responded as he handed us another printout, this time a resume. "Brenda, I called the cops to follow up on the break-in. I asked if there were any updates with their investigation. They said they were unable to locate Donnie and are still investigation the matter. So, I did my own digging. The reason the cops can't find Donnie Hensley is because that person doesn't exist."

"What do you mean he doesn't exist?" my mom asked.

"Donnie's real name is Mason Reed."

"You're playing, right?" Aunt Sherri asked.

"Why would he use an alias?" my mom asked. I just sat quietly, taking in the information given to me.

"I'm getting to that. What I passed out to y'all is an application to our company and his resume. I did a search on Mason Reed and this driver's license popped up." He handed each of us a printout of Mason's driver's license. We all gasp.

"Oh, my gosh!" my mom said slowly.

"I don't get it. If the cops couldn't find him—"

"How did you make the connection?" my mom asked, interrupting me but finishing my question.

"Brie, after you called me yesterday and told me Donnie or, Mason shall I say, changed his appearance, I alerted my workers. My girl that was assigned to watch the house last night took a picture of this man walking in front of your house early yesterday morning, not too long after Loyal left." Glen held up a picture on his phone.

I took the phone from him and enlarged the photo. "Yep, it's definitely Donnie. Bald and clean shaven just how Loyal described him," I said, as my mom took the phone from me. She nodded her head after looking at the photo, confirming it was Donnie.

Uncle Glen continued. "I ran his picture in our databases for face recognition, and Mason's driver's license pulled up with one hundred percent match. Now, that name stood out to me, which is why I went through our application files. Mason had applied for our company three years ago. He passed the first two interviews. A background check and medical disclosure was done prior to his last interview with Gerald. Gerald denied his application due to his mental issues."

"Mental issues! What mental issues?" Aunt Sherri asked.

"He's schizophrenic. He was also diagnosed with depression. As you all know, I can't have employees that have been diagnosed with any type of mental illness walking around with weapons training and fighting everybody."

"Of course, that's why Gerald didn't hire him," Mom exclaimed.

"Exactly! I think Mason tried to get revenge on him for not hiring him," Uncle Glen said.

"That kind of explains his weird behavior," I said, thinking back to when Donnie grabbed my arm.

"What weird behavior?" Mama asked me.

"How he could go from angry to happy in a blink of an eye. Like, the time he grabbed my arm. It would also explain some of the things he was saying at the time I got burned. He said something about protecting me and mama from our hurt and lost and taking the place of daddy. Now, it all makes sense," I said as I turned to look at Mama. "He was there to see our hurt and lost that day," I said with silent tears falling from my eyes.

"But why would it take him three years to try to pursue us?" my mom asked.

"I can answer that for you," Uncle Glen answered while he was on his tablet. "This is the police report from Gerald's accident. It does show Mason as the other driver. It also states that Mason was taken to the hospital for injuries. He complained of pain in his head. From there, he was institutionalized into a mental hospital."

"Why?" my mom asked.

"C.I.P.A." Uncle Glen replied, looking at Aunt Sherri. Aunt Sherri's mouth dropped open as she looked back at Uncle Glen in disbelief. She then turned to look at my mom and me.

"Congenital insensitivity to pain with anhidrosis. Basically meaning that he doesn't feel pain or temperature. He doesn't sweat when hot. It's a rare disease but—"

My eyes got bigger, my mouth fell open and I immediately covered my mouth with my hands. "He didn't get burned!" I blurted out, cutting off my aunt.

"What?" my mom asked.

"When the house was on fire, I got burned, obviously, but I was wondering why Donnie wasn't reacting to the pain. The flames were basically touching him, but he moved and talked normally as if it wasn't there. He didn't cough neither."

"Well, that could be why. He got burned; he just couldn't feel it," Aunt Sherri said.

"I honestly thought he was the devil," I said.

Uncle Glen stood up, closing his laptop and putting his tablet away. "I'm going to the police department and hand over my findings to the person investigating your case. In the meantime, ladies, if Donnie or Mason, whatever you want to call him... if he comes around here, you end him! Since he can't feel pain, that makes him extremely dangerous. "Brenda, did you make a police report yet?" Uncle Glen asked.

"Yea. Brie and I went down there yesterday."

"Okay, good. If anything should happen, it's self-defense. Have my number on speed dial and call me if anything goes down. You don't even have to say anything, just call me and drop the phone. I won't be too far away. Y'all hear me?"

"Yea Glen."

"Yes, Uncle Glen."

"I do believe Donnie is out for blood. Brenda, it's your call. Do you want me to leave my people out front to watch the house?" he asked.

"No! The sooner this is over, the sooner I get my life back. Let him come. I'm ready!"

15

After Uncle Glen and Aunt Sherry left, time seemed to have slowed down. I was not sure if it was because I was emotionally drained or just numb to the information we just received about Mason. I was certainly convinced that the experience I had with the house on fire was definitely the future. Everything about that experience made more sense now that I knew Mason couldn't feel pain. Like Uncle Glen said, just that part alone made him more dangerous. With my uncle pulling his guards from the front of our house, I knew it was only a matter of time before Mason popped up. I just wish I knew when to expect him.

I leaned back on the couch and stared at the ceiling. All the workers were gone now. The new security system had been installed. There were now sensors on every window and every door, motion lights set up around the house, and cameras located inside and outside the house. The windows had been replaced with shatter-proof glass, and the 65-inch TV had been replaced in the living room. The only thing that wasn't installed was the security screen door; unfortunately, that wouldn't be delivered until next week.

"Brie, you feeling, okay?" Mama asked while walking into the dining room. Mama had been on the move since everyone left.

"I guess I'm feeling a little nervous," I said as I got up and walked into the dining room to see what she was doing. There was a small safe sitting on the table, along with a bottle of wine and a wine glass that was half-full. I took a seat next to mama.

"That's understandable. This isn't an ideal situation to be in. Does the vision you had about the house catching fire make you more nervous?"

"I would be lying if I told you no," I said, putting both my elbows on the table and holding my head in my hands.

"You want some wine? It might help you relax a little."

"No, thank you," I replied.

"We'll be okay, Brie. All we can do is be prepared. Plus, you can handle yourself very well Brie. Did you forget about all the training your dad put you through?"

"I know mama, but that was three years ago. I haven't had any practice since Daddy died."

"You're thinking about it too much. It will come back to you."

"What good would fighting him even do? He can't feel pain," I sighed.

"Well, that's not going to stop me from having fun with him. I want to see him bleed for what he did to my husband. He may not be able to feel pain, but I want his death to be slow," she said as she pulled the safe towards her.

"And what am I supposed to do?" I asked.

"Just watch my back," she said as she punched in a pin number to open the safe.

"Oh! Before I forget, I bought some fire extinguishers. I put one under the sink in the kitchen, the other is in the hallway closet," she said as she took her gun out the safe and examined it.

"You about to clean it?" I asked.

"Nope, I cleaned it a couple of nights ago. I cleaned yours too," she said, side-eyeing me. I looked at her as though she'd lost her mind.

"Mom, I don't have a gun. Unless you're giving me Daddy's old gun."

"Nope. Your dad bought you a gun for your eighteenth birthday. When I told you he was planning on teaching you how to shoot, it was going to be with your own gun."

"Mama! Why didn't you tell me?" I asked. She shrugged her shoulders while loading her gun.

"I don't know. We were both going through something. I was miles away, and you were sitting at home blaming yourself for your dad's death. It just wasn't the right time."

"Well, where is…" I was cut off by her cell phone ringing. She looked at the caller ID and smiled.

"Hey Tammy! I haven't heard from you in a while; how you been?" She got up, put her gun in the holster of her tank top and took a sip of her wine.

"I know it's been way too long," she said while grabbing the safe and walking towards the hallway.

I shook my head. Perfect timing. It seemed like every time I needed to know something of importance, I always got interrupted. Tammy was my mom's best friend from childhood. She might be on the phone for a while.

I went into the living room to watch some tv, trying to take my mind off all the drama to come. I settled on a comedy. Thirty minutes into the movie, I still felt the same. The sound of the doorbell made me jump. I stared at the door for a moment as if I could see who was behind it. My heart was racing as I slowly got up to get the door. I was shocked when I looked through the peephole and saw Loyal. I opened the door with a smile.

"Hi! I didn't expect to see you so early," I said as I opened the door. He was holding three Tupperware trays. I gestured for him to come in. "You can sit that on the table," I said.

"I wanted to surprise you with lunch," he said as he sat the food down on the table. He walked over to me and embraced me in a hug. "You okay?" he asked.

"Yeah. I'm just stressed out with this whole thing dealing with my mom and her friend."

"Is there anything I can do?" he asked as he kissed my forehead.

"No. You being here is actually doing a lot."

"Brie, who's at the... oh! Hey, Loyal. I didn't know you were stopping by."

"How are you doing Ms. Taylor? I made us lunch. I wanted to stop by and bring it over before I went to work."

Loyal turns to looked at me. "Brie, I know I was supposed to come hang out with you this evening, but Ami called and asked if I could close tonight instead of coming in early. I have to be there in a couple of hours."

"Aww," I said, disappointed. Loyal was literally the distraction I needed from all the anxiety I was feeling. Loyal must have sensed my disappointment because he started caressing my back.

"Well, I hope y'all hungry," he said as he turned away to uncover the food. Mama and I took a seat at the table.

"Yeah! I'm always hungry for some good food. Did you make this?" Mama asked.

"Yep. I made us some toasted turkey club sandwiches, Mediterranean pasta salad and some brookies for dessert."

"What's a brookie?" Mama asked.

"Really mama?" I said.

Loyal laughed as he answered her question. "It's a cookie and brownie cooked together."

"Okay, so it's a cookie brownie. Why didn't y'all just say that? Y'all and your fancy names." I just shook my head, as Loyal laughed. "I've had cookie brownies before," my mom continued, as Loyal went into the kitchen to grab us some plates. "Y'all want some wine?" Mama asked.

"Sure, I'll take a glass," Loyal said from the kitchen.

"I'll take some too," I said. My mom cut her eyes at me.

"Oh, now you want some wine." She rolled her eyes up at me.

"What? It pairs good with the pasta salad," I said, trying not to laugh. "I'm going to get Loyal and I some wine glasses," I said while getting up, trying not to laugh.

"Don't worry, I got it," Loyal said from the kitchen.

I couldn't help but to smile. I followed Loyal with my eyes. I thought it was weird how quickly he got comfortable around me and my mom. He seemed to have memorized the way my mom had the kitchen organized. He opened cabinets to pull out plates and opened the drawer to grab utensils. He didn't have to search for anything.

I glanced back at Mama. She was watching him as well with a look of approval on her face. She caught me looking at her and mouthed, "Marry him, now!"

"Mama, stop!" I whispered. Loyal walked over to us, preparing to fix our plates. The food looked amazing. The turkey club sandwich had two layers. The bottom layer had turkey, tomatoes, cheddar cheese, bacon, slice of bread, then more turkey, bacon and lettuce. I could see a little of the mayo seeping from the side of the sandwich. The pasta salad was so colorful. It looked delicious as well. It was a glass Tupperware bowl full of penne noodles, grape tomatoes, sliced up cucumbers, red onions, spinach, sliced black and green olives, and feta cheese. The brookie looked soft and gooey. I couldn't wait to sink my teeth in that. Loyal handed us our plate and made his own.

"The pasta is tossed in Greek dressing I made from scratch," Loyal stated.

I took a spoonful of pasta into my mouth. It was so good, very flavorful. I really didn't like chilled pasta but, this, I was definitely going to have to get more servings of. Mama got up and poured Loyal and me some wine.

"Thanks, Ms. Taylor."

"Thanks Mama," I said. "So, you bake too?" I asked, sampling the sandwich.

"Yeah. I bake pies and cakes too. I make my own icing, but I don't do all that fancy decorating. Do you like to cook?" he asked me.

"Umm... I can cook but I wouldn't say that I enjoy it as much as you," I replied, taking a sip of my wine. I looked at my mom, waiting on her to embarrass me. She was taking a sip of her wine. She sat the glass down and smiled at me. I look up, rolling my eyes with a slight shake of my head. "Here she goes," I said to myself quietly as I forked up some pasta.

"Loyal, you should try some of her gourmet hamburger helper!" she said with a big grin on her face.

"Gourmet hamburger helper?" Loyal said, raising up one of his eyebrows.

"My mom hasn't even tried it yet." I looked at her with a scowl. "Anyway, I just spice it up a bit. Actually, it tastes pretty good," I told Loyal.

Loyal nodded his head up and down. "I want to try it. I love turning regular dishes into something new and amazing. What about you, Ms. Taylor; you like cooking?"

"I wouldn't necessarily say I like cooking, but I don't mind it. Now, don't get me wrong. I can throw down in the kitchen. That's how I hooked Brielle's daddy," she laughed. Loyal laughed and nodded his head, agreeing with Mama.

"Yeah, that's one way to a man's heart," he said, looking at me.

"What's the other?" I asked.

"Being you," he said, taking a sip of his wine.

I looked down at my plate, trying to hide the fact that I was blushing.

"So, in the words of my mother, are you two going steady yet?" Mama asked.

"Steady?" Loyal laughed.

"Mama, really! Who says that?" I laughed. "Nobody says steady anymore Mama."

"I said in the words of my mother," my mom laughed. "Well, how long have you two known each other?" she asked.

"I met Brielle when I started working at Ami's two years ago."

"Then, why is it that you two are just now starting to date?"

"Mama!" I said, shocked at her question. I almost spit out my wine. "Mama, I'm sitting right here, you could have asked me that in private."

"It's alright Brie, that's a good question. I've always been attracted to Brie," he said while looking at my mom, then turning his gaze to me. "I never approached you

327

because I was in a relationship. Just about a year ago, the relationship with south and we broke up."

"I didn't know that," I said.

"You wouldn't because you were too shy to ask."

"I'm not shy!"

"Then, what do you call it?" he laughed.

"Yea Brie, you do have a little shyness to you," my mom said, agreeing with Loyal.

"There's nothing wrong with being shy Brie."

"But, I'm not shy! Of all people, mom, you should know that. Just because I keep to myself don't mean that I'm shy."

"Well, I always thought you were shy until I saw how you handled rude customers. You had this like, 'try me if you want' attitude. I really like that about you," he said.

"Okay. Well, what about you? You seem shy too," I asked Loyal.

"Who me... no, I'm just observant," he said, taking a bite of his sandwich.

"Well, either way, I'm glad you two are getting to know each other but, you do know that one of these days, you two are going to have to start going on dates outside of this house, right?" Mama asked.

"Why? Are you getting tired of me and my cooking already?" Loyal laughed.

"No, not at all. It's just that if you keep cooking like this, Brie and I both are going to be dating you," Mama laughed, however, I didn't think that was funny. I couldn't believe she'd just said that. "Aww... look at Brie getting mad. I'm just playing girl. Wipe that frown off your face," Mama said as she stood up and picked up her plate. "I'm about to go back to finish what I was doing. Loyal, it was nice seeing you again and your food was delicious."

"Thank you, Ms. Taylor. Don't forget to try the brookie."

"Oh sweetie, I'm stuffed. I'll try it later, but thank you. You two enjoy your date!" she said as she turned to walk away.

"Sorry about that," I said to Loyal.

"What are you sorry about?" he asked, finishing off his wine.

"For all of her embarrassing questions and her statement about both of us dating you."

"Oh girl! Don't worry about that. I think your mom is funny. I like her; she reminds me of my mom. Wait until you meet her."

"Oh Lord, there's two of them?" I said, laughing.

"No... four. I have two sisters, remember. They all have my mom's personality."

"Yikes."

"Don't worry. You will fit right in, they'll love you," he said, caressing my hand. I looked at the table and started gathering all the dishes. Loyal got up to help.

"No, I got it."

"It's alright. I don't mind helping."

"Loyal, would you sit your butt down! I told you I got it. It's the least I could do. I mean, you did cook," I said as I picked up his dishes. Loyal raised up both his hands as if to surrender.

"Thank you," he said in defeat.

"You're welcome." I noticed Loyal smiling as I walked into the kitchen. "What?" I asked.

"That was that 'try me if you want to' attitude, wasn't it?"

"No," I laughed.

"You've already done so much. I just wanted you to relax before you have to go to work."

"That's nice of you. Thank you for being so thoughtful." Loyal looked at his watch. "I got about two hours to burn."

I got a little sad knowing that my time with him was running out.

"You know, I've never been yelled at on the second date before."

"Well, it's a first time for everything," I laughed.

After putting away the dirty dishes. I led Loyal to the living room. I let myself fall onto the couch and patted the seat next to me for him to sit. I snuggled up into him, as he put his arm around me and I un-paused the movie. I tried my best to get into the movie. *Jumanji* was one of my favorites. All I could do was count the minutes until Loyal left. He must have sensed it because he started caressing my shoulder.

"You want to talk about it?" he asked without even taking his eyes away from the screen.

"Huh?"

"Do you want to talk about it? I know something is bothering you. I can feel it. Your vibe is off."

"I just wish you didn't have to leave so soon."

"I know, but that's not what's stressing you out." Loyal turned to finally look at me.

"Nothing, I'm fine," I said with a smile, trying to look and act as normal as possible. It seemed like Loyal could see right through me.

"Brielle, let's not start this relationship off with lies."

"Relationship?"

"Girl! Don't act like you don't know where this is going. I know something is bothering you. You don't think I seen the side piece your mom had strapped to her or what about the car that was parked out front of your house; it's gone now. I noticed the driver never got out of the car. You got motion lights on the house now. Sensors going off when you open the door. What's gotten you so shaken up Brie?"

"Dang, you noticed all of that?"

"I told you I was observant. So, are you going to tell me what's bothering you?"

I turned my gaze back to the tv, trying to think about what to tell him. "My mom's friend is coming over."

Loyal looked at me as if he knew it was more to what was really going on.

"Brielle, your mom is strapped. Is this the friend turned stalker? The same guy that grabbed you up and broke into the house?"

"Yeah?" I admitted. Loyal was quiet. He took his phone from his pocket and was scrolling through his contacts. "What are you doing?"

"I'm calling Ami. I'm not going to work today."

I quickly snatched the phone from him before he could hit the call button. I couldn't let Loyal call in to work. Work would be the safest place for him. After our talk with Uncle Glen, I knew just how dangerous Donnie was. If what I experienced when I got burned was indeed the future, I didn't want Loyal anywhere near this house when Donnie showed up. I blamed myself for my dad's death for years. I would never forgive myself if something happened to Loyal because of me.

"Brie, what are you doing? Give me the phone back," he said as he reached for the phone.

"You really don't need to call in to work."

"What are you talking about? The same guy that is stalking you, grabbed you up, and broke into the house is coming by here and you expect me to go to work?" he said, raising his voice just a little.

"We'll be okay. Mama is expecting him. She's strapped, incase anything pops off. It's only for protection." Loyal was staring at me as if he was trying to search for the truth. I did tell him the truth, just a softer version for his sake. "Listen, if anything goes wrong, I will call you. Both me and my mama can handle ourselves. We will be okay," I told him, giving him back his phone. "Plus, I'm not even sure what time he's coming. It could be today or tomorrow.

All my mama told me is to expect him," I said, trying my best to sound confident as I gave him a small smile.

"You better call me the moment he gets here," he said, taking his phone back.

"I will!"

Loyal looked at his phone, checking the time before he put it back in his pocket. "It's time for me to head out," he said, standing up and pulling me up with him. I walked him to the front door, still sad to see him leave. He turned around, embracing me tightly in a hug.

"I mean it, Brie!"

"I know... I'll call you when he gets here," I said. *Please don't make me promise. I hate making promises I can't keep*, I thought to myself as he released the hug.

"Oh! Don't forget your trays," I said, getting ready to head to the dining room to grab them.

"No, don't worry about it, I'll get it later."

"Okay, well, be careful on your way to work."

"I will," he said as he kissed me on the lips. "Call me!" he yelled as he walked to his car.

I smiled as I closed the door and locked it. I went back into the living room and put on *Jumanji 2.* I was into the movie until the tiredness set in. Before I knew it, the tv was watching me.

16

I woke up to darkness. The tv must have turned itself off. The room was dark. I picked up my phone to look at the time. Ugh! 9:30 p.m. I couldn't believe I slept the day away. Right when I was about to put the phone down, a text message came through from Loyal.

Loyal: Everything good?

Me: Everything is good. I just woke up from my nap.

Loyal: Just checking.

I leaned back on the couch and stretched. Now, what was I supposed to with the rest of my evening?

"Brielle! You up?"

I jumped at the sound of her voice. "Mama! You scared me."

"I'm sorry, sweetheart. Didn't mean to startle you. I didn't know if you were sleep."

"I was. I just woke up. What have you been doing all this time?" I asked her. She took a seat on dad's favorite chair next to me.

"I fell asleep too. That tends to happen after you eat a good meal," she said as she turned on the table lamp beside her. We both tried to hide our eyes from the brightness of the light. It was blinding.

"No! Mom, turn the light off," I pleaded.

"I didn't know it was that bright. What time did Loyal leave?" she asked while turning off the light.

"A little after two. He had to be at work by 2:30."

"Is he coming by later?"

"No. I told him not to. I don't want him anywhere near this house incase Donnie shows up."

"You two never answered my question. Are you two together?"

"No but, according to him, that's where we're headed."

"Good. I like him for you," she said.

I couldn't help but to smile after getting my mother's approval. "Do you think Uncle—"

"Shhh!" my mom whispered, cutting me off. "You hear that?" she asked in a whisper.

"Hear wha…"

I quickly got quiet when I heard keys jiggling at the door. I held my breath, looking at Mama with a frown on my face. I was so scared, I could hear my own heartbeat. We both looked at the door. Nobody else had a key to our house except for me and Mama.

Mama turned the table lamp on just as the door opened. Donnie walked in and looked surprised to see us. He wore a black jacket, a black shirt with a cameo strip going across the front, dark blue cargo jeans and black Timberland boots. "I thought you two would be sleeping," he said casually.

"I know like hell I didn't get all this security installed in my house only for you to walk through the damn door," Mama said calmly, but I could hear the anger in her voice.

I stayed quiet. This wasn't my fight. I'd let my mom do all the talking. Her only request was that I watched her back, and that's exactly what I planned to do. I refused to let the vision of my mom's death become a reality. I already lost my dad because of Donnie. I felt like I lost him twice because of my most recent visit to the past. My world was already incomplete because of Donnie. I refused to lose my mother because of him too.

"Babe, I'm home!" he said with a dumb smile on his face. He stood with one hand on the doorknob as he stepped further into the house.

"How and when did you get a key to my house?" my mama asked, still sitting down in the chair.

"That doesn't really matter now... does it?" he asked calmly, closing the door behind him.

"Well, I suppose you're right," Mom said while sitting further up and scooting to the edge of the chair.

All the nervousness that I had was gone. It was game time. While Mama was talking to Donnie, I took the opportunity to slowly ease up over the couch. I casually started to creep towards the hallway. I wanted to grab the fire extinguisher, have it ready just in case Donnie decided to play with fire.

"You know it shouldn't matter that I have a key. This was eventually supposed to be my house too. Along with you, of course," he said, looking around where he stood. He started removing his jacket. "I had plans for us," he said, throwing his jacket on the couch in front of him.

"Well, plans change. Doesn't it Mason?"

Donnie smiled as he put both hands in his pants pocket. As of now, I was standing in the dining room facing Donnie. I was leaning against the wall, trying my best to hide the fire extinguisher between me and the wall as best as I could. Donnie hadn't looked at me once, all his attention was on my mama.

"Wow! I haven't heard that name in a while. It was Glen, wasn't it? He figured it out, didn't he? I knew it was a chance he would catch on. Damn, he's good. That's alright!" Donnie pulled a small silver object from his pocket and started flipping it between his fingers.

"He was next on my list anyway. I'll just pay him a little visit after I'm done here," he said just before he flipped the lid open on the silver object in his hand and lit the curtain on fire.

I quickly walked up to him and shoved the bottom of the extinguisher into his head as hard as I could. He fell forward to the floor. I immediately pulled the pin on the extinguisher, aimed and squeezed the handle, quickly putting out the fire he started. Donnie was still lying on the floor. We could clearly see the machete tucked into a strap that was tied to his back. My mom bent down and removed the machete, tossing it onto the floor behind the couch.

"You think I killed him?" I asked, sitting the fire extinguisher down.

"No. Evil people don't give us the satisfaction of dying fast. You just knocked him out but good job, Brie!"

I walked to the couch that hid the machete and placed the fire extinguisher next to it. "So, what now?" I asked.

"We wait for him to wake up."

"Do you want me to call Uncle Gen?"

"Not yet but you can grab your gun."

"Where is it?"

"There's a safe in your closet."

"Oh, that thing! I've seen it."

"The combination is seventeen, twenty-four, eleven."

Okay... seventeen, twenty-four, eleven," I repeated to make sure I got it.

Just when I was about to turn away, I noticed movement from Donnie. Before I could warn Mama, he knocked her off her feet. She fell, hitting her head on the corner of the coffee table that sat on the side of my dad's favorite chair. Donnie was quick to his feet while his eyes never left my mom; I knew what was coming next. I moved quickly, punching him in his chest and causing him to stumble back just before his foot could connect to my mom's side. I quickly stepped over my mom while delivering two more blows to the gut. Donnie was tall; all I could do was deliver body blows, try to knock him down to my level. I kicked his leg from under him, causing him to fall to his knees.

"Finally!" I said as I nailed him in his face twice. Donnie was slow. I was able to block most of his hits. He hit me in my head. My head went back, causing me to stumble backwards. I quickly regained my posture. I came back fast, grabbing his head and ramming it into my knee. He looked at me with blood running from his nose, and the same dumb smile was still on his face.

"You can't beat me!" he said while spitting out blood. "Just wait until..."

I spin-kicked him in his head, causing him to fall to the floor. I didn't have time to talk. Just as I was about to go to work, my mom tapped my shoulder, breaking my trance.

"I want in! Go get your gun."

I looked at my mom, quickly assessing her. She had a deep gash on the side of her face. "Are you sure?"

"Yeah," she said, letting Donnie get up. "Just hurry back."

Donnie may not be able to feel pain but damage was being done. He moved as if he was dizzy. Once he regained his balance, he reached behind him, trying to reach for his machete. After realizing it wasn't there, he rushed my mom, body slamming her against the wall and choking her with both hands. She grabbed his hands, dropped her shoulders, and brought her arm around, elbowing him twice in the face, breaking loose from his hold.

"Go now!" she yelled at me as she wiped some blood from her forehead with her arm.

I ran down the hall to my room, turning on the light. I hated leaving that man in there with Mama, even if she could defend herself. I quickly threw my closet door open and dropped to the floor. My anxiety was catching up to me. I could hear the beating of my heart again. I felt like I couldn't breathe in enough oxygen. My arms and legs were heavy, tingling from the lack of oxygen. I stared at the pile of clutter on the floor in the closet. I knew the last place I saw the safe was on the floor in the back of the closet. I started tossing out purses, clothes, shoes, box of tampons, and books.

I finally got to the back of the closet and the safe wasn't there. I stood up while putting my hands to my head, gripping my hair. Ugh! I knew the last place I saw it was on the floor. I tried to look on top of the shelves in the closet by standing on my toes, but I still couldn't quite see. I pushed all the clutter to the side and went back into my room to grab my desk chair.

After grabbing the chair, I turned back towards the closet and almost dropped the chair trying to shield my eyes from the glare of the sun hitting my dresser mirror. Still trying to fight my anxiety, I sat the chair down and started tossing things from the top shelf.

"I found it!" I said out loud to myself. I grabbed the safe and tried to remember the combination. "Seventeen, twenty-four, eleven," I said slowly as I turned the dial.

The lock popped open on the first try. I grabbed the gun and ran back into the living room. My arms and legs were still tingling and it hurt to breathe, but I wouldn't let that stop me. I reached the living room, and it was completely dark. I turned the hallway light on, relieved to find Mama standing over Donnie.

"Is he dead?" I asked, hopeful.

"It's hard to tell. This man is relentless. I broke quite a few bones, yet he still kept coming," my mom replied, still looking down at him.

"How long has been down?" I asked.

"A few minutes I think," she said as she turned to look at me. She was covered in blood.

"Mom! Is that your blood? Please tell me it's his."

"I don't know," she said as she wiped the gash on her head with the back of her hand. I saw more blood gushing out from the wound.

"Did you find the gun?" she asked.

351

"Yeah."

"Good, hold on to it. If he wakes up, kill him."

"Are you ok?" I asked her.

"Yeah, I'm just tired," she said as she walked over to the couch.

"Well, I'm calling 9-1-1. That's a bad head wound. It's bleeding too much," I said as I walked into the kitchen for the phone. I dialed 9-1-1, and a large thump sound caused me to look up. I threw the phone before I could reply to the operator. My mom fell to the floor, taking the table with her.

"Mom!" I yelled as I ran over to her. Her eyes were rolling back. There was blood coming from the back of her head. I tried to put pressure on her wound to stop the bleeding.

"Mama, don't go to sleep. Please don't go to sleep Mama!" I cried. I yelled for help until the room started spinning. I was in the air flying further away from Mama. I hit the wall and fell to the floor. *What just happened?* I thought as I looked at Mama across the room from me.

"Mama!" I tried to yell out, but it was only a whisper.

"She can't help you now!" Donnie said with slurred speech.

"Get away from me!" I yelled, trying to get up. A kick to my ribs caused me to fall on my face. I felt the moment my ribs broke. The pain that I felt when I tried to breathe was unbearable. I looked at Mama from teary eyes, as Donnie dragged me down towards him and straddled me. I tried my best to fight back, but the pain in my chest was too painful.

Donnie started choking me with both his hands around my neck, making it even harder to suck in air. He banged my head against the floor, giving me an extraordinary headache. I clawed at his fingers, trying to loosen his grip on my neck. I tried to reach for his eyes, but he was too tall. I tried my best to keep fighting, despite how weak I felt.

I looked over at my mom lying there lifeless. I thought about my dad. What's the point of fighting? My world was already gone. Donnie slammed my head into the ground again. My vision was getting blurry. My head felt like it was going to explode. The pain started to fade. I welcomed the darkness that started to surround me.

The sound of the front door opening awakened the fight in me, but it was already too late. I was trapped in the darkness. I could vaguely hear the commotion going on around me. I heard a loud crack. It was quiet, darkness was all around me, and all my pain was gone.

17

Water. I felt water hitting my feet. I heard waves. My eyes slowly opened to the brightness of the sun and the blue sky. I laid there enjoying the warmth from the sun. I sat up, looking at the ocean water as the waves hit my feet. I looked out at the beach as I dug my hands into the sand. I loved being at the beach. It was so peaceful. The sound of the waves was mesmerizing, demanding you to pay attention to it. It still amazed me to know that it was a whole other world underneath the waves.

"It's beautiful, isn't it?"

I slowly looked behind me with a smile on my face to find a pair of beautiful green eyes staring back at me. "Hi Grandma Kitty!"

"Hi baby," she said, returning my smile.

I turned around to look back at the ocean. "Am I dead?" I asked, already knowing the answer to my question.

"No sweets... it's not your time yet."

"Then, where am I?"

"This is your comfort zone. The one place in the world that helps you to unwind and give your problems to the Lord without you even realizing it."

"I love the ocean."

"I can tell," she said. She walked up to me and took a seat in the sand next to me.

"Where are my parents?"

"They are where they belong."

"How are you here?" I asked..

"I was told to come here… keep you company until it was time for you to go back."

"I don't want to go back. There's nothing left for me there but heartache.

"That's not true sweets. I was shown a glimpse of your future. You have so much to live for."

I got quiet. I just stared at the ocean, watching the waves crash onto the sand. I wanted to feel mad that I wasn't going to be able to stay and be with my family, but I couldn't. I felt so at peace here. "I just want to be with my parents."

"You will eventually sweets," she said while she rubbed my arm. Her hands were warm. I looked at Grandma Kitty. Her face so beautiful, her long black curly hair blowing in the breeze. She looked just as young as she did on the day I saw her in the shack. The only difference was that she looked happier now, more at peace.

"How did you do it Grandma? How did you make the choices you made back then?"

Grandma Kitty looked out at the ocean.

"My time was hard. It was unfair, it was scary and full of sadness and anger. I did whatever I had to keep the ones I loved safe. Either we were going to be safe together on earth or together with God." Grandma Kitty looked back at me.

"You see, child, that's the difference between you and me. I never lost my faith. With every disappointment I faced in the living world, my faith stayed strong. I knew I was gone be free with my babies one way or another despite what anyone would tell me. In my time, faith was all we had in a world of such hate. I never stopped talking to God and I let my faith lead me. You lost your faith when you lost your dad, didn't you? When was the last time you prayed?"

I couldn't answer her question. I just looked out to the ocean as I listened to everything she said. She was right. When Daddy was around, we stayed in church. We prayed together all the time and me, personally, I did feel closer to God back then. Once Daddy died, my life turned dark. It was filled with anger, guilt, sadness, confusion, and loneliness. I was mad at God for allowing my dad to get taken away from us. The last prayer that I heard was from Aunt Gracie at the family reunion, but I couldn't remember the last time I prayed myself. I looked down at the sand in my hand.

"Yes. That's the day I lost it. That's the day my whole world was turned upside down. I'm afraid I haven't spoken to God since that day."

"Sweets, you need God more when you're going through the hard times. Where do you think your strength comes from? Now, don't get me wrong. You also need to praise Him during the good times too, but I'm sure you already know that, right?"

"Yes ma'am."

"Good! Never stop talking to God, no matter how mad you are. Always remember, with God, all things are possible. Now, open your eyes!"

"Huh?" I was confused.

"Open your eyes!" her voice echoed.

I opened my eyes. All I could see was the ceiling. I look around, noticing I was in my room. I looked at the cupcake on my wall. The room was lit up by the natural light from the sun coming in from the window. It was all a dream. I looked at my arm. There was no burn, no bandages. Everything seemed so real. I wondered how long I had been asleep.

I got up out the bed, stretched, and make my way to the bathroom. After using the toilet and washing my hands. I walked to my mom's room and knocked on the door.

"Mama," I said as I opened the door. Her room was empty. Her bed was made up as if it wasn't slept in.

"Mama?" I went into her ensuite... empty. I went back into her room and looked at the clock on her wall. Nine-thirty in the morning, maybe she was in the kitchen. I went down the hallway, noticing the pictures on the wall were different. There were more of them. I took a moment to view the pictures. I smiled when I notice that Mama finally framed her degree. I read the inscription on the degree.

"What! Mama has a doctorate in psychology, this is a master's degree," I said out loud to myself. My mouth dropped open when I saw my name on the degree.

"This is mine! How could this be?" I started looking at the other photos on the wall. There was a picture of Mama holding two kids: a little boy and girl. They both looked to be about three or four years old.

"Whose kids are these? Mama would wait until I was grown to give me siblings," I said, shaking my head. I continued looking at the pictures. "What!" I said, holding my breath. *Are my eyes playing tricks on me?* CeCe was standing on the beach with a very pregnant belly.

I wonder who the daddy is? I thought to myself. I finished looking at the other pictures, hoping to find one with CeCe and her possible baby daddy. One picture caused me to come to a complete stop. My mouth fell open and I stared at the picture, making sure my eyes were not deceiving me. I carefully took the picture off the wall and stared at it more closely. It was me in a wedding dress, standing at the altar with Loyal. I smiled.

"I marry Loyal!" I said in disbelief.

I heard keys jiggle at the front door. I looked towards the door, still holding the picture frame. Once the door was open, I was blinded by the light. I couldn't see who was at the door. All I could make out was a shadow.

"Brielle, open your eyes!"

"Aunt Sherri?" I said aloud, still looking at the shadow figure standing at the door.

"Wake up Brielle," I heard again.

I closed my eyes and took a deep breath. Pain was what I felt. Every part of me was starting to hurt. I slowly opened my eyes to more bright lights. Aunt Sherri was smiling back at me with tears in her eyes.

"Brie! Baby, you're okay!" she cried.

I tried to turn my head to look around, but my neck hurt bad.

"No, no, no, baby, don't turn your head. You're at the hospital," Aunt Sherri said through happy tears. She had a look of relief on her face.

I let the continuous stream of tears fall from my eyes. I didn't want to come back. I was happy where I was. There was nothing left for me here except pain. The agonizing pain I felt from every breath I took. The horrible pain I felt in my throat whenever I swallowed or turned my head. Not to mention, the worst headache I'd ever experienced in my life. My head hurt so much that my eyeballs were throbbing, but what hurt worst of all was the pain of knowing my parents were gone. I started shaking uncontrollably. I was furious.

"Why did you bring me back!" I yelled through all the pain. "I was fine where I was! Why did you bring me back? You should have left me!" I screamed.

"Doctor! We need to sedate her!" Aunt Sherri yelled from my bedside.

"You should have let me die!" I screamed. I started kicking and hitting whomever I could. I knocked the IV pole down and I pulled the leads off my chest. I pulled the IV out of my arm. "Leave me alone!" I yelled, as three nurses rushed me, holding me down while the doctor gave me a shot. I fought through all the physical and mental pain I was feeling, hoping that all the pain would take me back to where I was. I fought and fought until darkness and quiet surrounded me.

18

Beep… beep… beep. *What's that noise?* I slowly opened my eyes. The light in the room instantly gave me a slight headache. I closed my eyes again, hoping it would relieve the pain. Nope. I opened my eyes again, trying to figure out where I was. My vision was a little blurry. I coughed, trying to clear my throat and tensed at the pain in my chest.

"Hey Brie, take it easy."

Uncle Glen's voice startled me. I didn't realize he was sitting next to me. "Where am I?" I asked in a little more than a whisper.

"You're at the hospital."

"What happened?"

"You don't remember?"

I shook my head no but instantly regretted it.

"Are you in pain?" he asked worriedly.

"Yeah," I replied with my eyes closed. I felt Uncle Glen pick up something next to my hip. A moment later, I heard a nurse on the speaker.

"Did you need something?"

"Yes, Brielle Taylor is awake. She says she's in pain."

"Okay, I'll be right over."

"What happened?" I asked.

"Well, baby girl... there was a break-in at your house. You and your mom put up a good fight, but the two of you were hurt pretty bad."

"Where's mom?"

Before he could answer, we were interrupted by a knock at the door. A nurse entered the room wearing dark blue scrubs.

"Well, look who's awake! Hello Brielle, my name is Faith. I'm your nurse until about three o'clock today. I was told you were in pain?" Her name made me think of Grandma Kitty and our conversation.

"Yes," I answered.

"Can you tell me where?"

"My head and my chest."

"Okay. That's to be expected. On a pain scale from zero to 10, what would your pain be?"

"Eight."

"Okay, I'm going to give you some pain medication through your IV. You should feel some relief in about a minute or so."

After giving me the medicine, she grabbed the blood pressure cuff and tried to put it on my left arm. I quickly snatched my arm from her.

"Not this arm! I have second-degree burns," I said in a little more than a whisper.

"What burns?" Faith and Uncle Glen asked together.

I looked down at my arm. The burns were gone. I looked at the palm of my hand, just smooth skin all the way down. "Oh... I'm sorry. I guess I dreamed it," I said. I continued to look at my arm, trying to make sure I didn't overlook the burns. The nurse proceeded to take my vital signs.

"Everything looks good. The doctor will be in shortly," she said while walking to the door.

"Yes, thank you," Uncle Glen replied before the nurse walked out the door. "What's the last thing you remember Brie?"

"I remember mom laying on the floor covered in blood. I remember a lot of blood. Is she dead?" I asked with tears already threating to fall.

"No, baby girl. Your mom is fine. She ended up having a blood transfusion but for the most part... that's pretty much it besides some stitches."

I felt my body relax the moment he told me she was alive. Instead of tears of sorrow that had threatened to fall from my eyes, it was tears of happiness. I still had my mom. I closed my eyes, silently thanking God for the good news.

"Baby girl, why don't you get some rest. I'm going to go make some calls. Let everybody know you're up."

"Okay," I said, as he got up and kissed my forehead before walking out.

I was tired, but I couldn't sleep. I was in deep thought trying to put together the missing pieces of my memory. I did, however, remember the beach and the conversation with Grandma Kitty. I just stayed there, remembering the feel of the sun on my skin, the water hitting my feet and the feel of the sand between my fingers. I could still hear the calming sound of the waves. I just stayed there in my comfort zone, enjoying the moment. This time, I was alone. Grandma Kitty was nowhere to be seen. I could just stay here forever. If this place made me feel like this, I could only imagine what heaven was like.

"Hello Cupcake."

I knew that voice anywhere. "Hi Daddy!" I said as I got up from the sand and walked to him, giving him a hug. He kissed me on my forehead, and I opened my eyes.

"Daddy!" I cried.

"Shh, it's ok now. Don't cry Brie," he said as caressed the side of my face.

"But, how are you here?" I asked, touching his face. I wanted to make sure I wasn't dreaming. His soft, coffee-brown skin. His green eyes stared back at me, his curly black hair with a low fade on the sides. He looked exactly the way I remembered him.

"You were d.."

At that moment, I forgot what I was going to say. A flood of new memories started flashing in my mind. On my eighteenth birthday, there was no reason for my dad to leave the house. It was that time of the month for me, and I had just got back from the store. I was upset that I couldn't find the box of tampons I had just bought. I ended up finding it on the floor next to the closet.

Uncle Glen, Aunt Sherri and CeCe came over that day. We barbequed, had cake and opened gifts. My dad bought me a gun and a safe to keep it in. We danced and played games that entire night; it was one of the best days of my life. My old memories were becoming fuzzy; they were starting to fade.

"I'm so glad you and your mom are ok. I don't know what I would have done if I would have lost you two," he said as tears ran down his cheeks.

"Is Donnie in jail?" I asked through my own tears.

"Who's Donnie?"

"I... I don't know. That's not the guy who hurt us?"

"No. His name was Mason. He broke into the house looking for me. It seems he wanted revenge for me not hiring him," he said as he sat down next to me. "He's not in jail. You don't have to worry about him anymore. I lost it

374

when I walked in. Seeing your mom on the floor and him on top of you, choking you. He was dead before I realized what I was doing. I just thank God I got there when I did," he said, squeezing my hand.

"Me too."

"Knock, knock," my mom said, peeking in from behind the door. "Look who I found!" she said as she walked in the room with Loyal following behind her. He had flowers and a white teddy bear in his hand. He walked to my dad, greeting him.

"Hi Mama!" I greeted her, as she kissed my cheeks and took a seat on Daddy's lap. She had on a light-blue sun dress, and she wore her hair straight with bangs. She hid her wounds very well.

"How are you feeling?" I asked her.

"I feel great now that you're awake."

Loyal sat the flowers and teddy bear down on the nightstand next to the bed. "Hi beautiful," he said as he kisses my lips. "How are you feeling?" he asked.

"Fine, now that this medicine kicked in," I replied while tugging on the IV cord.

"Good. I hear you're finally going home tomorrow," Loyal said.

"Finally! How long have I been here?"

"Today's the third day," my dad answered.

"I was out for three days?"

"Heck yeah, you were!" Aunt Sherri replied as she entered the room with Uncle Glen and CeCe.

"Brie! This was the longest three days of my life," CeCe said, running to me. She softly laid on my bed next to me and gave me a soft hug and a kiss on the cheek.

376

"Hi CeCe. You good?" I asked.

"I'm good but I been worried about you! How are you feeling?" she asked.

"I'm fine."

"Brielle, we had to keep you sedated girl. You were very combative. Beating on the nurses, throwing equipment, you pulled out your IV," Aunt Sherri continued. "You punched one nurse so hard in the face, she just about quit her job."

"No, I didn't... did I?" I asked, shocked at what she was telling me. Everyone in the room nodded their heads. Loyal had a big grin on his face, as if he were proud of me.

"I don't remember," I confessed

"Yeah, baby girl, it's true. You were unconscious when you arrived. When you came to, you were fighting,"

377

Uncle Glen said. He was leaning against the counter holding Aunt Sherri from behind.

"What was wrong with me?"

"You had a concussion and three broken ribs," CeCe said, still lying in the bed with me.

"Yeah, Cupcake, you got to take it easy when you go home. It's going to take a while for your ribs to heal," Daddy said.

"Oh, she will. I'll be there every day to make sure she's following doctor's orders," Loyal said, holding my hand.

I nodded my head yes as I looked around my hospital room. I got a warm feeling in the pit of my stomach. For some reason, I was excited about the future. I looked at everyone in the room and smiled. I didn't know why but, for the first time in a long time, I felt complete. I

felt like I got a second chance at life.

Made in the USA
Las Vegas, NV
25 January 2024

84866501R10213